SOCCER MOM

A Romantic Suspense Novel

EVE LANGLAIS

Killer Moms #1 - A Bad Boy Inc. Spin-off

CHAPTER ONE

THE MEETING WAS GOING ABOUT AS WELL as expected, which was why when Carla's phone rang —a lively song called "Fireball", which could only be one person—she announced, "Excuse me a moment while I take this call."

Mr. Ramirez looked none too pleased, but he didn't say a word.

Sliding her phone free from her pocket, a press of her fingertip answered the call. "What is it, *mijito?*"

"I scored. Three times!" Her son's excitement burst from the speaker, and she beamed.

"That's amazing! So those new shoes we got are working, then?" She'd splurged and bought the expensive soccer shoes for her boy. He deserved something extra given that her work was going well and he'd gotten As on his last report card. The budget didn't appreciate the stretch, but it was for a good cause. Her son, Nico, was an up-and-coming soccer star.

"I am super-fast now, Mami. I wish you could have seen me score."

"Me too, *mijito*. Next game. I will be there cheering loudly."

"When are you coming home?" The plaintive query tugged at her heart. Nico hated when she traveled out of town, but sometimes, her job required it.

"My flight leaves tonight, so I'll see you in the morning." Not entirely true. She was actually only about an hour's drive away. However, she would have to pick up her car at the airport and drop off the rental paid for in cash. After she wiped it down, of course.

"Love you, Mami."

"Love you more," she sang before hanging up. How she adored her boy. She hated being away from him, but sometimes, duty called.

She slid the phone into her pocket before turning her attention back to the fellow she was meeting with. The knife she held against Ramirez's throat hadn't moved at all during the call, not even when she juggled the phone to answer.

It helped that Ramirez was duct taped to a hotel chair.

Good thing she'd already sealed his mouth shut before answering. Ramirez seemed like the type to not respect a mother taking an important call from her son.

"Where were we?" she mused aloud. A sham.

Carla always knew what was going on. She had to in her line of work. "That's right, you were going to tell me where you stashed the money you stole."

The big man, in a suit now showing sweat stains in the pits, and sporting a ruddy complexion that implied an unhealthy lifestyle, glared. She could just imagine what he'd say if she ripped that tape off his face—after he was done yelling. She'd bought the good stuff. The kind that didn't come off even if soaked.

Which was why she didn't bother tugging. She'd heard it all before.

"*Fucking bitch, I dare you to hurt me.*" She never was one to refuse a dare.

"*Cunt. I'm going to mess you up something fierce.*" Actually, she messed *him* up something good.

And then there were the pussies who begged. "*Please don't kill me. I'll do anything you want.*" Those were the worst types, the ones who'd sell their own mothers to make a buck or save their skin. Carla made the world a better place by taking them out.

It didn't take the file she'd read beforehand or the drink she'd shared with Ramirez to lure him into her trap to know that his ego, and his misogyny, couldn't fathom a woman causing him harm. Even when he woke tied to a chair a few hours after she'd fed him a mickey in his drink, he held on to his arrogance and demanded she let him go.

The idiot thought he was in charge. He'd soon learn. Men always underestimated her. She knew what they saw when they looked at her. Petite Latina, weighing a hundred and ten pounds with a slim and trim figure, who, with her heritage, must surely be ready to suck the cock of any guy who bought her a drink.

Little did they know that she was more likely to cut it off.

Carla crouched before Ramirez and dragged her knife down his chest, flicking each button on his shirt along the way until the tip of the blade pressed against his groin.

"You know, there's a reason why my boss specifically gave me this job." Carla was the one they sent to do the dirty work. "I have no problem hurting you. You remind me of my father." Which wasn't a nice comparison. The man who'd raised her was a violent drunk. He'd also stolen money from those less fortunate. Such a shame he stumbled onto those railroads tracks just before the three o'clock came roaring past. They'd saved money on the funeral because there was so little of him left to bury.

Carla pressed a little harder, digging the tip of the knife deep enough that she knew he felt it. "You ready to tell me where the money is?"

Ramirez glared. Daring her.

Without changing her expression, she shoved on the hilt of her blade. It pierced fabric and stabbed him in the balls.

Ramirez attempted to scream from behind the

tape. Tried to thrash, too. It didn't get him anywhere. Another reason she invested in the sturdy shit.

She wiggled the knife before pulling it loose. Blood immediately stained his slacks, and the man whimpered. No longer so brave.

Resting on her haunches, she waited for him to calm down and focus. She hummed patiently, not bothered at all by her actions. Her ability to feel had been broken a long time ago. Nowadays, only a few people could get her to care, and this scumbag wasn't one of them.

Ramirez calmed to a hiccupping whimper.

Dangling the blade in front of his face, Carla said, "Ready to tell me now?

It took a few more jabs of the knife before he frantically nodded. Once the tape was ripped free, in between sobs and snot, Ramirez spilled where he'd stashed the funds he'd embezzled from the church.

What kind of scum stole from a place that helped the poor? The kind that didn't deserve any more chances.

Carla relayed the information she'd learned to her handler, who confirmed the money was being transferred back to the proper owners before giving Carla final instructions.

There was no sympathy in Carla's eyes, no regret in her soul when she sliced Ramirez's throat. She let him bleed out on the hotel carpet as she went about creating the scene of his robbery and murder.

The cops would mention in their report the missing cash and credit cards from his wallet. The empty bottles of wine. The glass with the remnant of a drug. What they wouldn't find was any trace evidence such as fingerprints or hair. Not real hair, at any rate.

The only thing they'd have would be some video footage. The hotel cameras would have caught Carla accompanying him. A blonde woman with heavily made-up features and a padded shape with high heels skewing her height. The wide-framed sunglasses added an extra layer of concealment.

Scene set, Carla stripped out of her disguise and cleansed her face with the wipes she'd brought, stuffing those used tissues into her purse. The wig joined it, along with the dress she'd worn. The padding in her bra and around her hips deflated with the jab of a pen. It also went into the bag. From her large shoulder purse, she pulled out black leggings and a long-sleeve T-shirt. She dressed quickly.

She slung the purse strap around her torso before leaving by the balcony door, climbing with ease down the various outdoor terraces until she reached the ground. She'd chosen this place specifically for its design.

With quick steps, she left the area. Not that she expected anyone would follow or even care. Ramirez had signed his own death warrant with his actions. Sadly, another would probably take his place. Scumbags abounded, and Carla was one of the few people who took them out.

For a fee. Assassins didn't work for free, although this assassin would offer a discount if the target were an asshole who deserved it.

Having planned her route beforehand, it didn't take long to reach the jogging path that lined the city's sluggish river. The purse with the bloody knife and all her gear was quickly weighed down with a rock and dumped into the water.

By the time the news reported on the murder of financial advisor Tony Ramirez, Carla was pulling into her driveway.

A much richer woman.

CHAPTER TWO

ALL THE MONEY in the world wouldn't save her from the stupidity and pettiness of others. Carla held in a sigh as the various soccer moms and dads continued to argue about who was to blame for the team's coach deciding to accept a new position that allowed him to marry his long-distance girlfriend and move out of state.

Yes, it was inconvenient, especially with the big regional game coming up. It came as a surprise that Coach Mathews would quit so close to that event. But, at the same time, he wasn't making a ton of money being a coach in the public school system and even less volunteering as the soccer coach for some inner-city kids.

Couldn't blame him for accepting the position at a private school that probably offered him benefits. Despite the disruption Mathews had caused, Carla wasn't in the camp of parents who argued he should be blackballed from coaching again, even if his actions made her son upset enough that he'd pushed away his dessert the previous night. Given it was Nico's favorite, blue Jell-O and whipped cream, it showed how much the change affected him.

And more change was about to hit.

The league had already hired a temporary replacement. That worried Carla, especially since no one had heard of this Moore fellow before. Apparently, the new guy wasn't local. He'd just arrived from the West Coast and landed the position.

The parents—whispering and ranting among themselves—all wondered about the new coach's credentials and worried about their precious darlings. Except for Carla. No worry on her part. She already knew that Nico was the best player on the team, and even the most inexperienced of coaches would recognize it soon enough.

As the parents gathered in the school's gym, all having arrived early for the team's parents' meeting, and continued to argue and lament, Carla checked her phone. Her message-less phone.

It had been six months since her last job. Longer than usual. Enough that she'd contacted her handler to ask if she were being passed over for some reason.

Mother, the name her handler went by, had replied with, *"Business is slow. Be patient."* In other words, none of the jobs needed a hitwoman. Pity.

Carla didn't want to be patient, though. She was only a million dollars away from having enough to retire from the killing game and not worry about her or Nico's futures. She kept her riches socked away in an offshore account, untouched but available. One day, she'd start laundering it in her direction, but until then, she kept building that nest egg. An egg that wasn't quite ripe enough yet.

But money wasn't the only reason she fretted. Boredom plagued, as well.

The life of an insurance adjuster didn't offer much excitement. Mostly paperwork and more paperwork. Investigations into whether a claimant truly deserved the money they applied for or if they'd faked an injury or staged a catastrophic event to their home/vehicle. It never ceased to amaze Carla the lengths people would go to in order to get a payout they didn't deserve.

She actually did quite well in her job. Her record of detecting fraud had earned her one of the top spots in the company. Which meant, more paperwork.

Given her so-called normal life consisted of working and being a mom, she didn't often get a chance to truly let go and get her adrenaline pumping. Other than her job, her last thrill had occurred more than ten months ago when she helped out a friend of hers with an ex-boyfriend problem. Carla hadn't gotten to kill anyone on that trip, though—and came home with an embarrassing bruise because she'd not seen the threat posed by an old lady. That adventure had ended up with her bud, Audrey, finally getting rid of the dick-head threatening her. Fist pump. But then her friend, a woman she called "sister," did the unthinkable.

Audrey fell in love.

It still blew Carla away that Audrey had let another man into her life after what her ex had done. Carla would certainly never let a guy get that close to her again. However, despite all the reasons not to, Audrey got herself a boyfriend—another mercenary to boot.

Talk about a killer couple.

They'd just completed their first mission together, and the agency they worked for—titled, interestingly enough, Bad Boy Inc., a worldwide realty company—helped them out with daycare, cover, and protection.

Kind of cool. Especially the part where Audrey didn't have to hide who she was from her lover.

No one knew about Carla and her double life except for those she trained with and Mother. A few Bad Boy operatives knew Carla by face and first name, but for their sakes, they'd better keep their mouths shut, or they'd be sleeping at the bottom of a river. And if a body of water weren't handy? There was always a construction site somewhere pouring concrete footings.

Carla wasn't dumb enough to let wet panties rule her life, not since Nico's dad. That wasn't to say she was celibate. She enjoyed sex. On her terms. Casual hookups that involved satisfying an urge and nothing more.

Clingy men who tried to tie her down found them-selves brushed off and blocked. She had no time for that kind of shit. She didn't need a boyfriend or a husband. As for those that might claim Nico needed a father? Fuck 'em. Fathers weren't always the be-all and end-all for a child's wellbeing. In some cases, a father intentionally stood in the way of happiness. Hence why her daddy had stumbled on those tracks.

A sudden hush filled the room, and Carla lifted her head to see the cause. A man had entered, taller than she was but not quite six feet she'd wager. He had brown hair that waved thickly on top but was trimmed short on the sides. He sported a close-cut beard and mustache that followed a jawline that wasn't quite square but held some strength. His collared, white polo shirt and casual khakis didn't scream *athletic*, yet he appeared fit enough, judging by the forearms bulging from his sleeves.

He cast a glance over the room, his eyes—a shade of blue-gray—not resting on anyone until his gaze met Carla's. He paused a moment where they exchanged a stare before he looked away and spoke. "Good evening. As I am sure you're all aware, Coach Mathews has resigned."

"More like he let some chick crack a whip," someone heckled.

"Be that as it may, he is now gone, and I've been chosen as his replacement to finish out the season. My name is Philip Moore." Said with a deep timbre that had her shifting in her seat with a frown.

"We don't care about your name. What're your qualifications?" The bold demand came from Fergus, a hulking fellow in plaid and denim with narrow-set eyes and a soft double chin. His son looked nothing like him or the boy's mother, which made Carla wonder if Mrs. Fergus had a secret.

Moore stood at ease, feet slightly apart, and addressed them. "I started playing soccer at the age of four. Given my father was a diplomat stationed in Europe, once my talent was noticed, I was enrolled in a soccer academy. I played all throughout school and received a soccer scholarship for college. I was considered talented enough that a few European leagues headhunted me."

"Why did you stop playing?" The query came from Josee King, the team goalie's mom.

Carla could have answered because there was only one reason a pro athlete ever stopped playing.

Moore pointed to this knee. "Ripped ligaments. The doctors fixed them, but it ended my career."

"What's your experience teaching a team?"

The questions went on and on, but Moore had an answer for each of them, even the sly one, "Will your wife and family interfere with your duties to the team?"

"I'm single and don't even have a pet, so I can dedicate all my off-time to the kids."

More than one single mother—and father—along with the not-so-single ones, perked up at the answer.

The meeting eventually turned from pinpointing his jock size—not quite but close given that Sally Ann remarked he'd need a bigger set of athletic gear than Coach Mathews—to the team itself, the remaining practices of which there were only two, and the upcoming final game.

Carla only paid a little bit of attention to the details. Once the season was done, win or lose, she and Nico were going on a trip. She'd already booked the time off work, put aside some money—because insurance adjuster Carla didn't have access to the millions in the offshore account—and promised Nico they'd go see the ocean.

Eventually, the questions petered out, and Moore called an end to the meeting. "Nice meeting you all. See you at practice tomorrow."

As the parents filed out of the gym, Moore shook hands with each of them but kept conversation short. Carla tried to sneak past but accidentally caught his gaze.

He smiled and said, "Hi. Philip Moore." He held out his hand.

She could have rudely swept past—it was late, and she wanted to get home—but that wouldn't do Nico any favors. She mustered a smile and ignored his outstretched hand. "Hello, Mr. Moore. I'm Carla Baker."

"You're Nico's mom."

The man had obviously read over the team roster. "So nice of you to step in to help the team."

"Always a pleasure to be able to do my part to encourage youth."

What a load of bullshit. Did he seriously mean it? She didn't roll her eyes, but she did check his expression for any hint of mockery. Didn't spot any, but that didn't mean anything. No one spotted the assassin in their midst either.

"I should get going," she said. "Nice meeting you."

"See you tomorrow, Mrs. Baker."

She didn't reply or correct him. It was Miss, not Mrs. She headed out the door and restrained an urge to glance at him, even though she was sure he stared. The prickle between her shoulder blades never lied.

Let him look. But she'd break his hand if he touched.

CHAPTER THREE

PHILIP WATCHED Carla leave and stared longer than was probably seemly. In his defense, he was a red-blooded male. He'd have to be dead to not notice that she was an attractive lady. Late-twenties in appearance, fit, with tanned skin and dark hair and eyes—all hinting at a Latina heritage. Short, too, which meant his less than stellar five-foot-ten made him taller than her.

Yeah, he'd noticed how she would fit nicely against him, but that didn't mean he did anything about it.

Given he'd been driving all day to make this meeting, he quickly said goodnight to the last straggling parents and left—without accepting an invitation for a drink. He had no interest in the women who brazenly eyed him and hinted at their availability. In his world, he preferred a woman play a little harder to get. A chase made the prize more worth it.

Heading out to the parking lot, his gaze went immediately to Carla—as if she were a magnet—caught in a group of parents, probably tearing his resume to shreds. Let them. Despite his lack of actual coaching experience, they'd soon see his mettle on the field.

Walking to his car, he couldn't help but cast glances at Carla. Her impatience showed, and she quickly edged herself out of the gang and moved quickly before anyone could draw her back in.

As she traversed the lot to a navy blue minivan parked at the far end, he noticed a car on the street slowing down. Odd given the lack of streetlights or stop sign.

The passenger window opened, and a muzzle poked out.

"Get down," he yelled.

Luckily, Carla wasn't one of those idiots who had to ask why.

She hit the ground even before the first crack of gunfire. Whereas Philip started yelling and waving his arms. Doing his best to distract.

Other people screamed *"Oh my God, they're shooting at us."* and *"Get your fat ass out of my way. I need to grab my gun."*

The rapid fire kept going, spitting bullets in Carla's direction. She scrabbled on hands and knees around the edge of her van as glass rained down around her.

From his left, he heard a yelled, "Motherfucking gangbangers. You want lead. I'll give you lead."

Bang. Bang. Philip looked over to see Fergus firing a shotgun at the car. Too far away to actually hit it, but it helped. The shooting stopped, and with a scream of rubber, the car sped off.

Amidst the sobbing of one woman and the excited chatter of others, Philip bolted in the direction of Carla's van and almost sighed in relief as she peeked over the hood.

"Are you hit?"

"No." Which did nothing to lessen her scowl. "Lucky for me, they don't know how to aim."

Which was a miracle given the number of bullets fired.

"Fucking thugs," Fergus huffed as he reached them, shotgun still in hand.

"Thank you for chasing them off," Carla said. Was it him, or did she seem reluctant to say it?

"Ain't nothing." Fergus tipped his ballcap. "We got to look out for each other against those criminal elements." The big man cast an eye at her van. "Want me to call you a tow? My cousin might still be on shift."

"No. I've got this." Her lips pursed as she yanked out her phone and waved it.

"You get a discount on your rates working for the insurance company?" Fergus asked.

She shook her head. "Nope, but I know the best shops to ensure I don't get gouged."

"Honey! Come back over here. I want to leave

before they come back." Fergus's wife's shrill voice carried, and the big man shrugged. "Guess I better go."

"Shouldn't you stick around to give a statement to the police?" Philip asked.

"To say what?" Fergus sounded genuinely curious. "This kind of thing happens all the time."

Apparently true, since the police who arrived shortly after barely batted an eye as they wrote an incident report. It was Philip who asked, "Any chance of catching these guys?"

The older cop, with gray in his wiry hair, shrugged. "No license plate. No description. Not much to go on."

"Mrs. Baker could have been killed."

"But she wasn't."

"What about the fact it happened on school property? They could have hit a kid," Philip argued.

"But didn't. No one was injured, which means in the grand scheme, it isn't as important as the crimes where people are hurt," the police officer stated.

"That's insane," Philip snapped. "I thought we had laws against gun crimes."

"We do, but here's the deal, buddy. Yes, we could write up a report about an illegal firearm discharge, which is a serious crime. We could investigate. But unless we get a solid lead, don't expect it to get very far. The chances of finding the guys are slim to none. People in this neighborhood are tight-lipped. Not to mention, if we write up a report and pursue this, then we'll have to write one on that parent who shot back.

Firing a gun within city limits is a crime, even if in self-defense."

When Philip would have blustered some more, Carla put her hand on his arm and shook her head. "It's not worth it." Then, to the policeman, she said, "Thank you, officer. If we're done here, I'd like to get home to my son."

However, despite her wishes, leaving had to wait a few more minutes as she dealt with the tow truck that hooked up her van. When she would have caught a ride with the guy, for an extra fee, Philip intervened.

"I'll drive you home."

Carla cast him a glance and frowned. "No need."

"Yeah, there is." Because he wasn't sending her off with a guy who leered at her ass when she reached into her van to grab a few things that she'd stashed in her oversized purse. "Come on. My car is just over here."

She pressed her lips together, and he could tell she was ready to refuse again until the tow truck driver opened the door to his vehicle, and the stale stench of cigarette smoke wafted out.

Her nose wrinkled. "Fine, I'll catch a ride with you." She didn't sound happy about it and looked even less happy in his car. She sat ramrod stiff in the passenger seat.

While she might not be pleased by the turn of events, he, on the other hand, was intrigued. Unlike most people, she'd kept her cool during the shooting and remained calm after. More annoyed at the inconvenience than frightened. Made a man wonder if this type of thing had happened to her before.

"Have you lived here your whole life?" Philip asked, pulling out of the parking lot, the only other vehicle remaining that of the police, who had their dome light on as they filled out paperwork.

"No."

A short, terse reply. Philip didn't let it deter him. "I'm from Pasadena."

"Good for you."

His turn to frown. She wasn't making this easy. "I guess you're feeling a little shook up over what happened."

She finally turned to look at him. "Is there a reason you feel the need to make small talk, because I don't do small talk."

Neither did he, usually. "I just thought we'd get to know each other."

"Why?"

"Because we'll be seeing each other often."

"No, you'll be seeing my son. As his coach. I will be the chauffeur that brings him and screams obscenities at the other team from the sidelines."

He gaped at her. "You're joking, right?" It might be sexist of him, but he had a hard time imagining a pretty woman like her cussing like a sailor.

She proved him wrong. "I never fucking kid. Now, are we done with the useless chitter-chatter? You are really making me regret not catching a ride with Bubba. Next light, turn right."

He maneuvered the car into the turning lane as he asked, "Do you have a problem with me? I know I'm not Coach Mathews but—"

"Coach Mathews was a moron, and his only saving grace was that the kids liked him. You were handed a winning team and have two practices and one final game to not fuck up. Think you can handle it?"

"I thought I could, but geezus, now you're making me wonder about my choice of accepting the job." Because if all the parents were like Carla, he might just turn around and go back home to Pasadena.

An irritated sigh burst from her. "Listen, I don't know what you want from me. You harassed me into accepting a ride—"

"I did not *harass*." Merely strongly suggested.

"—and I was fine with that. But this whole attempt to..." She waved a hand.

"Be friendly?" he supplied.

"Whatever it is. You're wasting your time. We don't need to be friends for you to coach my kid. As a matter of fact, it's better if we're barely acquaintances."

"Can I ask why?"

"Because I don't need the other parents claiming I'm screwing or blowing you to get my kid ahead."

The car swerved, probably because her words shocked him.

She laughed. A low, throaty sound that did things to his body he should better control.

"Nobody is going to think we're, um, intimate just because I'm nice to you," he stated.

"You've obviously never coached a kids' team before. There are some that will assume we're involved because Nico gets more play time than the others. Next light, turn right."

"Why would he get more time on the field?"

"Because he's good. You'll see. And if you want to win, you'll need him. But some people are blind when it comes to their kids. Think their shit don't stink."

"And you're not blind?"

She snorted. "I know my boy's faults. Nico is a slob and sucks at math. But he is a star on the soccer field. However, not everyone will admit it."

"So, if I play him to his full potential, you think the other parents will assume we're sleeping together?"

"Well, yeah. Especially now."

"Why now?"

"You gave me a ride."

"Because your van was full of bullet holes."

She smirked in his direction. "Don't let facts get in the way of a good story. Next practice, I expect I'll run into some catty mothers who think I beat them."

"Beat them at what?"

"Getting into your pants."

He didn't swerve this time, but he did shake his

head. "No matter what you think, I'm not trying to seduce you."

"Good thing, because I'd have to hurt you if you tried." Said with such a serious note.

"Do you threaten all the men who flirt with you?"

"Yes."

Was she into women? The fact that she had a son meant nothing. "Just so you know, I have no intention of sleeping with you or any of the other mothers on the team. I'm just here to help the team out as a favor."

"Your lack of interest won't stop them from trying."

"Then they'll be disappointed."

"Not really. Say no too many times, and they'll assume you're gay, which means you'll be fending off a few of the dads."

"I'm not sleeping with anyone!" he exclaimed, still not entirely sure how this conversation had devolved into...insanity.

"It won't matter." Spoken quite smugly.

"I was asked to coach. I said yes. No one ever said it would involve parental drama."

"What drama? Just telling you how it is. Consider yourself warned. Turn left."

"What do you do when you're not avoiding the nonexistent advances of your son's coach?"

"Insurance adjustor."

"That's interesting."

She uttered an unladylike snort. "No, it's not. It's

boring. Sometimes mean. People hate me on principle, but it pays the bills."

"And Mr. Baker?"

"If this is your subtle way of fishing, then Nico's father is dead."

"I'm sorry."

"Don't be. He was an asshole. The world is a better place without him. I'm the townhouse with the weedy lawn out front."

He pulled to a stop at the curb. Carla barely waited before opening the door and spilling out.

"Thanks." She slammed the door shut.

"See you tomorrow," he shouted through the glass.

Her only reply was the swish of her hips.

And a challenge.

Which he accepted.

CHAPTER FOUR

THE MOMENT CARLA walked inside her house, the canned laugh track caught her attention. Why sitcoms felt a need to fake laughter, she never understood. Either the shit was funny, or it wasn't. The artificial audience noise didn't seem to bother Nico.

She preferred to watch documentaries, enhancing her mind. Although she had let her sisters convince her to see a few superhero movies. The antics of men in tights amused—and she coveted the bat of the crazy blonde in *Suicide Squad*. As for the humor of that actor Ryan Reynolds when he wore that black and red suit... she could only aspire to those heights of sarcasm.

Entering the living room, she found her son asleep on the couch, the television moving from unrealistic family drama to a commercial for whiter teeth. In her line of work, you often had to blacken them so they wouldn't shine at inopportune moments.

There was no sitter to pay. Not anymore. At twelve years of age—by like three days—Nico had declared himself old enough to stay home alone if she were only gone for a few hours. Given the cost of having someone watch her television and eat her food while Nico tended himself, Carla agreed. Hell, at even younger than twelve, she had minded herself and her brother while cooking for her older sibling, too.

For a second, her mind strayed to Pablo. He would have been twenty-six if he'd lived. At times, looking at Nico, Carla caught glimpses of her brother. The glinting humor in the eyes, the round cheeks. In some ways, Pablo lived on in Nico.

As for the rarer glimpses when her son looked just like his father? Her heart ached. Not because she missed Matias. That asshole better be burning in Hell for what he'd done. Mistreating her with words and his fists was bad enough, but when she'd finally had enough and left? He'd killed her family.

Mother. Two brothers. He'd even hunted down her best friend when he didn't get the answers he wanted.

She'd danced on his grave when he died of a gunshot to the head. A victim of gang violence the police said. A much too easy end, given she'd hoped to see him suffer.

But with Matias dead, at least she didn't have to worry about him coming for Nico. Her son deserved better in life.

She knelt by the couch and stroked the dark hair

that Nico insisted on growing—because it was cool—out of his face. He stirred and mumbled, "Mami."

"Hey, *mijito*. Sorry, I'm late. The meeting ran longer than expected." She lied rather than stress him. He'd find out about the shooting soon enough, but she'd rather not make an issue of it now. Let him sleep. "Move your snoring butt off the couch. Time you went to bed."

He'd grown much too big for her to carry, but she did support his sleepy frame up the stairs to his room, the walls painted a vivid yellow and blue to match his favorite soccer team in Brazil.

Pulling back his *Star Wars* comforter, she tucked him in and placed a kiss on his brow. "Night, *mijito*."

"Love you, Mami," he said drowsily, turning his cheek into the pillow, already back asleep.

Only once his door was closed did her expression turn hard.

Someone had shot at her. Intentionally? She couldn't be sure. Fergus had been correct that the west end of the city was prone to outbursts of violence. The soccer field wasn't in one of the nicer suburban areas. The school itself was flanked on one side by warehouses. The parents had complained for years that businesses were being run only yards from school property, but the alternative was bussing their kids across the city.

The idea never got enough votes, and so the school remained, stuck in the middle of a neighborhood that had long gone to hell; where the only green space was the massive field that the school managed to hold on to and maintain. An anonymous benefactor paid for its upkeep. Pity she couldn't claim it on her taxes.

Given those facts, there existed the possibility that it was a crime of happenstance. If so, it was an odd one. Because why randomly shoot at her? A lone woman posed no threat. On the contrary, the gangbangers usually preferred to harass those who dared to be out at night.

A shame she hadn't had her gun handy; however, the bulge of it was hard to hide in the warm summer months when clothing consisted of slim jeans and a T-shirt. With the speed at which the shooting had occurred, she'd not had time to reach into the dash compartment of her van or under the driver's seat to pull her piece. Probably a good thing. How would she explain to Fergus or the coach that she was not only legal to carry, but also a crack shot?

She still remembered the first time she'd held a gun. More than eleven years ago.

"You want me to shoot?" Carla exclaimed, looking at the gun nestled in the palm of her hand. The weight of the weapon was less than expected. A thing that could kill should drag down her arms. It would surely smother her soul.

Her instructor, Mother—real name Marie Cadeaux —made a noise. "Yes, I expect you to shoot. What else would you do with it? Club someone on the head?"

Lips curved into a teasing smile, Carla held up the gun. "It might not be heavy, but it would do the trick."

"If you're close enough to hit, then the enemy is close enough to hit back."

Not to mention, most people who brought a gun to a fight would use it. "Fine. You made your point." Carla held it aloft one-handed, feeling kind of gangster.

"Not like that, idiot," Mother said with a shake of her head. "Hold it with two hands. You don't want the recoil smashing it into your nose. Ask Meredith how that feels."

Back for some refresher training, Meredith, an older woman in her thirties—which seemed ancient to Carla at twenty—with striking red hair and Southern elegance, grimaced. "I only did it once, and that was enough. Listen to her when she says hold it with two hands. Especially if you don't want to get blood all over your shirt." Meredith placed herself into a shooting stance, both hands around the grip of her weapon, and aimed at the target, her expression serene behind the safety glasses.

Bang. Bang. Each bullet hit the head of the target.

Carla recoiled with each retort. Guns were something bad people used. Assholes like Matias, who used one to kill her family.

How could she possibly think of firing it?

Mother placed her hand over Carla's. "Why are you afraid?"

"I'm not afraid."

"You're lying. I can see your entire body trembling."

"Guns kill."

"No. The people holding them do."

"I don't know if I can do this." And she didn't just mean the gun.

When Marie had first approached Carla after the death of her family, she'd been grief-stricken and flitting from motel to flophouse to women's shelter. She'd escaped the bloodbath only by accident. She'd been at a doctor's appointment with baby Nico, who at six months, was due for more shots. She'd returned with a cranky baby to flashing lights and horror.

The nightmare didn't end that day. Not only did her entire family end up in the morgue, she'd also lost her home, her belongings. The police had cordoned off the entire house. She couldn't even get a change of clothes because the whole place had been ransacked and was the scene of a crime.

She'd stayed with a friend until the day she noticed Matias parked outside. Watching her.

Waiting.

He could have easily dragged her back to his place and beaten her. She had, after all, had the nerve to leave. But that wasn't Matias's way. He wanted her to crawl back and beg him. Beg him to take her in because she had no other choice.

Matias had killed Carla's friend the following day, even though Carla had left.

Terrified, she went to the police, who claimed they could do nothing until Matias acted.

"He killed my family!" she cried.

"We have no proof of that," was their reply.

Carla tried contacting the FBI, promising them testimony in exchange for safety, but she didn't know enough about Matias's drug dealing to make it worth their while.

So, when Marie Cadeaux, whom she'd later call Mother, approached her, waiting for her outside the women's shelter, she'd been skeptical.

"Hello, Carlotta. My name is Marie Cadeaux."

"How do you know my name?"

"I know many things, such as the fact I can help you."

Carla looked at the beautiful woman standing taller than most men, with her glossy, ebony skin, and her hair pulled back into a tight bun. How could this model-esque woman help?

Only one thing came to mind, and Carla's lip curled. "I am not whoring myself."

Marie laughed. "I should hope not. Your body should never be used to bargain for anything. What if I said I could give you a new life?"

"I'd say what's the catch?" Because nothing was ever free.

"The catch is, you work for me."

"Doing?"

"Odd jobs."

"*You'll have to do better than that.*" To this day, Carla didn't know why she'd stood there talking instead of walking away.

"*I run a group for women. Mothers, actually. It's exclusive, and by invitation only.*"

"*So you're like another shelter?*"

"*Not quite. Think of me more as a rehabilitation option.*"

"*I'm not an addict.*"

Marie snorted. "*I wouldn't make this offer if you were.*"

"*Why me?*"

"*Because you don't deserve to live in fear. Because one asshole shouldn't have that much power. Time for you to get your life back.*"

Speaking of fear... Carla saw Matias roll up in his car, the rumble of the muffler rousing Nico from his nap in the stroller.

"*I can't.*" She gripped the handle and began to push.

The woman put a hand out to stop her. "*I think you have to. Because, let's be frank with each other, if you don't do something, we both know what will happen. You'll eventually go back to that bastard over there because you'll run out of places to hide. But your return won't make him happy. He will beat you. Probably beat your son. Might even kill you both.*"

"*I will never go back,*" Carla spat.

"*If you don't, then he will kill you. And then where will little Nico be?*"

In the hands of his father. A fate worse than death.
"How do you know his name?"

"I know everything there is to know about you, Carlotta Lopez." The name she'd owned before she changed it to Carla Baker.

"You've been spying on me."

"A friend told me about your situation. I can help."

The rev of an engine drew her gaze, and she saw Matias sneering at her while his buddy behind the wheel laughed.

A touch on her arm drew her attention back to Marie.

"Don't become another statistic."

It burned in her gut, but Carla knew the woman was right. She'd end up dead, and if Nico didn't die with her, he'd end up in a system that didn't care, and the boy would most likely follow in his father's criminal footsteps.

"What do you want from me?"

Turned out, Marie wanted a mercenary. She took in women abused by life and the system, all of them mothers, and gave them a chance to take back their power. To make a difference, and make money doing it.

"Try it," Mother crooned a year later as they stood in the gun range nestled on over a hundred acres somewhere in Canada. "Fire the gun. Just once. See how it feels."

Carla bit her lip and inwardly cringed. *I hate guns.*

I hate guns. *She closed her eyes when she fired, and yelped as the gun in her hands leaped.*

"There. I did it." *She placed the weapon on the counter.*

Mother shook her head, her expression disappointed. "I didn't take you for a coward."

"I'm not a coward," *was her hot retort.*

"Then stop acting like one. A gun is a tool like any other."

"I don't see why I need to know how to use one."

"For the same reason I taught you hand-to-hand combat and computer hacking. I'm giving you life skills."

At that, Carla let out a sound. "I'm not an idiot. You're training me to be a soldier."

"And your problem with that is?" *Mother arched a brow.* "Don't you want to be able to fight?"

"You haven't said what I'll be fighting."

"How about anything you want? What if I said you could save other women like yourself, those caught in bad situations?"

"By killing," *Carla said, gesturing to the weapon.*

"Sometimes." *Mother didn't lie.* "We both know some people are too wicked to live. But there are other ways of taking down evil. We need to find out what your skill is."

Because it certainly wasn't knife work or seduction. As for code-breaking, she got bored. Carla did enjoy the hand-to-hand stuff, but her size often put her

35

at a disadvantage. Leverage was all well and good against larger people with no skills, but pit her against someone with the same training and a few extra inches and pounds, and it was all over. She had the bruises to prove it.

"Maybe I'm just not cut out for this."

"You want to quit?" Mother arched a brow. "Go ahead. I won't stop you. Take Nico and leave if you want. I won't force you to do anything."

"I have nowhere to go."

"Is that your only reason for staying? Then how about I put your mind at ease. You want to go, then I'll help you find a place and a job."

Carla pursed her lips. "I never said I wanted to quit. But I think it's becoming clear I just don't have any aptitude for the stuff you're seeking." She'd certainly failed all the home décor classes they had her taking.

"I'm not done trying yet. Are you?"

She heaved a sigh. "No." Carla gripped the gun, blinking back the vision of blood-stained walls. The memory of Matias holding a gun against her forehead, the metal muzzle digging into her flesh, him threatening to shoot.

The gun wasn't the thing she feared. It is only a tool.

Carla gritted her teeth and aimed again. Bang.

The hole in the torso winked daylight.

"I hit it." Surprise lit her words.

"Again."

She held the weapon steadier this time, sighting along the barrel, firing.

The chin got a dimple.

The next shot, she gave it a nose. Then a cyclops eye. A few more rounds, and then she was reloading. Firing again. Finding a certain serenity and balance in controlling the gun. Satisfaction when she hit her target.

Turned out, shooting was her thing, and she began to lose her fear. Gained confidence she'd never enjoyed until then.

A few months later, with one of her new friends watching Nico, she was back in the hood. Head held high. No longer a victim cowering at every noise.

She boldly knocked on a door, and when Matias opened it, she calmly raised the gun to his forehead.

He sneered. "If it's isn't the puta, back to beg forgiveness."

"Does this look like forgiveness?" Carla waggled the gun.

"You won't shoot me. You're soft."

"I was. Not anymore." Carla shook her head as she stared at him, his body tattooed all over, the signs of hard living already marking his features despite his young age.

"Get on your knees and beg, puta. Beg for my forgiveness, and maybe, just maybe, I won't kill you."

He threatened her like he had so many times before. But there was one difference now...

She felt no fear. No urge to bow. She saw him for the

mean and petty asshole he was. A man who would never change. Who would continue to hurt. The gun steadied in her grip. Her resolve hardened. "Never again, motherfucker."

It took only one bullet.

Just one.

People never knew it was her. They assumed a gang hit. She let them. She stood in the large crowd at his funeral and was smug inside at the hate and spit thrown at his coffin.

She'd taken evil out of the world. And it felt damned good.

And, as it turned out, Mother was right. Carla did have a knack for something. Vigilante justice.

When the law couldn't act, and evil flourished...*I am the person who puts a stop to it.*

Or, as Nico jokingly called her when she smashed a spider to death, "You're a killer mom."

Little did he know how close he was to the truth.

CHAPTER FIVE

THE WEATHER WAS perfect for Philip's first practice as the coach. The grass was dry, yet not brittle. The sun shone, but the temperature stayed in the low seventies. A light breeze moved air enough to keep everything refreshing. It would help when the kids began to sweat.

So many kids. They'd arrived in singles and pairs. Some walking onto the field with their equipment in a bag over their shoulder. Others dropped off by parents, not all of whom stuck around to watch.

Adults he could handle. The kids, though? Ranging in size and height, they were sitting on the ground, looking to him for guidance. Kind of jarring because it drew him back to when he used to play and had sat on the grass listening avidly to his coach's wisdom, waiting for the whistle to blow so he could play.

A whistle hung around his neck. Now, he was the coach. The role model.

In other words, he'd better not screw up, especially since he was being judged, not necessarily by the kids themselves, but by the parents who stayed to watch. They hung around the edges of the soccer field, sitting in their fold-up chairs, muttering among each other. Except for Carla.

She leaned against the hood of a car, not so much watching him as taking in the entire area around. What was she looking for? Did she fear another drive-by? After what had happened the night before, he couldn't blame her. He'd be keeping a wary eye out, as well. He didn't want any of the kids getting hurt on his watch.

He didn't spend too much time talking. Attention would wander if he droned on. He kept it basic: introduction, expectation, a joke that got the boys snickering, and then, onto the field.

For his first practice, Philip put them through some endurance tests, sprinting, crunches, and pushups. This would give him a good indication of who could handle double shifts on the field, and who would run out of gas and lag if the game got tough. Once he'd gotten them sweaty and their muscles primed, he ran them through some pylon drills. Passing, kicks on goal, carrying the ball downfield.

It quickly became obvious how this team had gotten as far as it did. For the most part, the kids were decent, they had the basic skills, knew what to do on the field, and yet that wasn't why they were playing in the final game. They had a star player. Nico Baker. A boy who looked a lot like his mother with his dark hair and tanned skin.

Despite Nico having talent, he wasn't a diva about it. He didn't grumble when he had to take turns. Didn't catcall if someone missed a pass. He appeared to be a genuine team player.

As for his mother, she didn't demand star treatment for her son. Philip didn't get a single email or phone call from her explaining how her precious angel needed special consideration.

She didn't have to ask. Nico earned it on his own with his athleticism.

If Philip were honest, though, Carla's son's immense talent wasn't the only reason he approached her once practice ended. But it did give him the opening he needed. "Can I talk to you for a minute?"

She turned to face him, taking her gaze off the street, and he was struck anew by her beauty. A natural one that required no artifice. Even dressed in faded jeans and a sweatshirt, she held herself poised, yet at the same time seeming prickly.

Unlike some of the other mothers, she didn't simper or flirt. She boldly said, "What is it? I kind of want to get Nico home to shower the stink off him."

"I don't stink," her son yelled as he neared them, a giant Freezie in hand. Apparently, each practice and game, a designated parent brought some treats for after.

"You do so smell," she retorted.

"It's manly," exclaimed Nico as he tossed his gear into the trunk of the rental.

Carla shook her head. "Sweat is not manly."

"Depends on the kind of sweat." The moment the remark slipped past Philip's lips, he regretted it since a shield came down over her face, blanking her expression.

"What can I help you with, Mr. Moore?" Ouch. Reduced to a mister. So much for getting on a friendlier footing.

"I wanted to ask if you've thought about having Nico play at a higher level."

"You talking about the national team? He's too young."

"Actually, I was talking about the Yaguara Academy. It's a school that caters to boys playing soccer."

"I know what it is."

"And? He really should check it out."

"That's by invitation only."

"I can get him that invite."

Her arms crossed, and her lips pursed. "That would be cruel since we can't afford it."

"There are ways of mitigating the cost." Which could run into the thousands of dollars.

"Ask for charity?" Her lip curled. "No, thank you. He's fine where he is."

"He's wasting his talent. He should be playing with kids who are closer to his skill level."

"Getting him into a more competitive environment means more stress. He's just a boy."

"A boy who could have a professional future."

For a moment, her face brightened, the pride of being a mama to a prodigy shining through before extinguishing. "I'd prefer he concentrate on school."

"Who says he won't? The best athletes out there are the smart ones who are educated. And the academy is all about ensuring that the kids' minds are exercised along with their bodies."

"His previous coach never said Nico should play higher." A stubborn rebuttal.

"Your previous coach probably knew if he lost Nico, his team would rank close to last place. I'll wager your son is the only reason this team has been winning."

"Nico is a team player."

"Never said he wasn't, just that he should be playing on a team better matched to his abilities. Think about it. I can get him looked at. And, as for cost, there are scholarship programs available."

"You think he'd qualify?"

"The boy is good. The academy would be lucky to have him."

She chewed her lower lip in a way that made a man want to chew on *her*.

"Maybe."

Which was the best he was going to get.

He watched her get into the rental car with her son

and drive down the road before pulling out his phone and dialing. When the call was answered, Philip said, "She didn't bite."

There was a pause. "Is it money?"

"Partially, which ties into her pride. She won't accept charity. The boy is talented, though."

"Told you he was. He's wasting his time there. They both are," his boss replied.

"Perhaps you should try contacting her and speaking to her directly."

"You have met her, right?" was the wry reply.

"The word stubborn does come to mind."

"Try harder. I want that boy here, at my academy, playing on a proper team."

"I don't know if she'll want to move."

"Then find a way to convince her."

Philip hung up and rubbed his jaw. That might be harder than expected.

CHAPTER SIX

THE COACH'S words spun around in Carla's head as she left the soccer field. Nico could be playing for Yaguara Academy. The big leagues. Not exactly money-making at his age, but Moore was right when he said it was a stepping stone to greater things. Like a scholarship to a good college or university, even a career. Soccer might not pay much in the USA, but over in Europe, her son could be a star.

A star that, if accepted into the academy, wouldn't be sleeping down the hall. Or giving her goofy grins in the morning. The academy was over eight hours away by car, meaning, he'd have to board. She'd lose her son.

She understood that Nico would eventually move out. Children weren't meant to live with their mothers forever. But the idea of losing him at twelve ridiculous.

Which meant if they pursued this, they'd have to move.

Moving didn't frighten her. She had no attachment to her townhouse or even her things. She kept the most precious items in a box. Pictures for the most part, and her mother's rosary. Not that she believed in religion. God hadn't been listening when Matias gunned down her family.

I'm not moving. Moore was probably just saying he could get Nico an invite to try out. The man obviously didn't get that Carla wasn't interested and thought he could butter her up. It wouldn't work.

Still, he'd managed to frazzle her, enough that she didn't notice the SUV trailing her for a few miles. But it became pretty obvious when it ran a red light, causing people to honk.

She peeked in her rearview mirror and noted it a few car lengths behind. Not tailgating. Not doing anything untoward. Could be a coincidence. People were impatient and ran reds all the time.

Training had taught her to never trust coincidence, though. Without using a signal, she turned a sharp right, and her son squealed.

"Damn, Mami, are you turning into a stunt driver?"

"Don't use that kind of language," she absently chastised, glancing again in her mirror.

The SUV followed.

"Damn is not a bad word. They use it on the radio and television all the time."

"It is too a bad word."

"What about darn?"

"Kind of the same thing."

She turned again. Left. Right. Her son thought it was a game and held on to the bar overhead, yahooing before continuing his argument. "You use it and the f-word all the time."

"I'm an adult." With a foul mouth. No denying that, but that didn't mean she let her child use the same language.

"That's not fair."

"That's life, *mijito.*"

When she slammed into the parking lot for the grocery store, she fully expected the SUV to pull in behind her. It slowed, and she stared at the tinted windows until it passed.

"I thought I was supposed to shower," Nico complained, looking at the store. "I hate shopping."

"We need milk." And time to see if the SUV returned.

Half an hour later, with a few bags of groceries and a grumbling tween appeased with the purchase of some snacks, she kept a sharp eye on the parking lot, then on the vehicles behind her as she drove home.

No one suspicious appeared to be parked on her street. She'd notice since she kept a journal of the cars that frequented the area. Just like she knew what time her neighbors worked.

Her paranoia had only grown over the years with the more jobs she did. She'd been living here a while. Too long, some might say. She worried about her cover being blown. A woman in her line of work had enemies. None that should know her true face. However, that assumed she'd not made any mistakes on her jobs.

Have I been compromised?

Only once Nico was in bed did she head to her tiny office with its regular-looking laptop sitting on an MDF desk bought at Walmart and assembled with much swearing. Duct tape covered a spot where the pressed wood popped because she'd overtightened a screw. She pulled the shade over the window before she plopped into the wooden kitchen chair.

Opening the lid to her laptop, she ignored the sign-in box. She plugged a pink skull USB into the side, hit a series of keys, and waited for the KM icon to appear. The KM standing for Killer Moms, the agency she did mercenary work for.

Clicking the icon brought up a different sign-in box, and she tapped in her credentials, the username an apt *Soccer Mom*. All the agents had aliases. Frenemy Mom was Audrey. Cougar was Meredith. Then you had Hockey Mom and Tiger. There was even a MILF Mom, which Lolita bore with pride. She had, after all, chosen it, given that her specialty was seduction.

All the mothers had their own code name, specialty, and cover. None of the active agents lived in the same town, but if help was needed, they were all ready to drop everything and fly to the rescue.

Carla didn't think she needed help, not yet. However, she did have questions. Things she couldn't ask regular folks.

The USB didn't just give her log-in access to the KM network, it encrypted all her activity so that if anyone watched, they'd see Carla surfing a few shopping websites and checking out threads on a mommy forum. All a sham because she was, in fact, browsing her secure mailbox. Still empty. No new jobs.

The lack of work wasn't why she put in a call to Mother, a call with no video, just voice.

It took only a minute for a reply.

"Hello, my darling daughter. How is my grandson?"

"Nico is great. Coach thinks he's got enough talent to play with the big boys. He also got an A in algebra."

Code for "It's safe to talk." If it weren't, she would have said, "He failed a Spanish quiz."

"An A? I might have to send him some of my special cookies." The proper reply that meant Mother could talk freely, as well, and Carla could drop the act. She dove right into the problem. "I think my cover might be compromised."

"What happened?"

Carla told her about the drive-by shooting and the SUV that had appeared to be following her.

Mother took a moment before asking, "Could it be a coincidence?"

"Maybe."

"What's your gut say?" Mother didn't accuse Carla of being paranoid. In their business, you could never be too paranoid.

"My gut wants me to wear a piece." And shoot at the next person who looked at her funny.

Mother tsked. "If anyone sees it—"

"They'll ask questions. I know," Carla grumbled. "But I don't like it. I had Nico with me in the car when they followed me today."

"And they were brazen enough to be seen? Seems kind of sloppy, if you ask me."

"I agree. It doesn't sound like pros." Because pros would have set up a high-powered rifle with a scope and taken her out from afar.

"Could it be you caught someone's attention with your actual job?"

"Someone with a beef over not getting insurance? Possible." People could get very irate when you wouldn't hand them money.

"Do you want me to relocate you?" Mother would if Carla asked. She never took chances with her operatives. KM might be an agency of killers, spies, and mercenaries, but it was also a tight-knit family.

"Not yet."

"Then what do you need?"

Assurance that her son was safe. "I don't know. If this is random, then things will stop on their own." If it weren't, Carla would hunt them down and shoot their asses.

"I don't like *if*'s. I want you and Nico safe." Because despite Nico being no relation, Mother had known him since he was a baby, and she wouldn't let anyone harm him. "Tell you what. Let me talk to my contacts out there. See if I can find out if something is going on."

"Guess it could be a scare tactic." Kind of dumb, because if Carla caught them, they'd die. There were no second chances where her son was concerned. She wouldn't have him threatened.

"If these are intimidation tactics, then you'll soon receive a warning."

After that, talk went to business with Mother grumbling, "Of late, all we've gotten is a ton of interior design work. Nothing else."

Killer Moms was the hidden part of the business. Publicly, KM—which had offices around the world—provided interior design services for the elite. The rich unknowingly let trained spies into their homes, which in turn increased KM's knowledge network.

Carla was one of the few who didn't work directly for the KM agency. Probably because her sense of style involved the use of white paint, no colored feature walls, and basic furniture.

Since she lacked the artistic talent, she'd ended up in the insurance gig instead, which suited her much better. But not being directly involved didn't mean that Carla got left out of the underground agency that only hired women—mothers, to be precise. KM believed in offering training and employment only to those who had nowhere left to go, those whose lives were in jeopardy, usually because of bad romantic decisions, and individuals who would do anything—even kill—to keep themselves and their children safe.

What did KM do with those they recruited? Just about anything they wanted. They offered education—which, for those who'd barely gotten a high school diploma like Carla, meant options in the real world. They taught life skills. Money management. How to defend against an attacker. Loading and unloading guns in the dark. Filching information from secured networks. How to bake a cake from scratch.

If a trainee made it through all the courses—and not all did, some were retired before they even got into the field—then they became an elite agent. A spy. A mercenary for hire. And, in Carla's case, a killer.

Which was ironic, given how weak and afraid she used to be.

New Carla would have never fallen for Matias and his violent bullshit. However, she didn't regret being old Carla, because it had given her Nico.

For the most part, the KM agents were sleepers. Living normal, mundane lives. But at least once a year, without notice, Mother called and offered a job. Anyone could say no. Mother never forced the moms she took in. However, refusing to act got you kicked out of KM. Which, for some, was fine.

Many settled into their new lives with ease and got comfortable. Happy. Not everyone wanted to risk their lives on a mission. Even if the money was crazy good.

Carla was one of the moms who thrived on the danger. Who socked the money away, ensuring her future.

And she wasn't about to let some asshole ruin it for her.

The next morning, her son was less than impressed when she insisted on taking him to school herself.

"Why can't I ride my bike?" he whined from the front seat. "Only babies get driven by their mommies."

"It's supposed to rain later. Maybe even thunder-shower." A lie. She'd not even peeked at a forecast.

"I'm not gonna melt." His lower lip stuck out in a mighty sulk.

"Stop complaining and be out front after school. I'll pick you up, and we'll go out for dinner."

"Why?" he asked, suspicion in his gaze. With good reason. Dinner out was for special occasions.

She dropped another fib. "Mommy got a promotion, and we should celebrate."

That brought a smile to his face and a promise to meet her out front at four.

Only she ran late getting there. Not by much. Five minutes because the repair place that had her minivan had tried to overcharge her, and she'd ended up arguing with them.

That five minutes almost cost her, though. As she drove up the street to Nico's school, she saw him on the sidewalk, standing only a few feet away from an SUV. Possibly the same one that had followed her previously. The passenger door opened, and a leg appeared.

Since she couldn't exactly start shooting in a school zone, she did the only thing guaranteed to draw attention. Carla slammed her hand on the horn, and the loud beep drew Nico's gaze. The guy in the SUV stepped out, his leather jacket and bandanna a bad sign. She slid her hand between her seat and the center console for the gun she kept tucked there as the guy reached for Nico. She stepped out of her van, gun tucked out of sight, ready to shoot despite the few curious parents milling around. The thug lost his chance as her son jogged towards her. She quickly tucked her gun back into its spot and grabbed her phone.

While Nico got into the passenger seat of the van, she snapped an image of the vehicle's license plate. She'd run a search on it later.

First... "What were you doing talking to strangers?" she harangued her son.

"I didn't do it on purpose. They pulled up and asked me where the nearest gas station was."

"You should have gone into the school. What have I said about staying safe?"

"I didn't get in the truck. Geez, Mami." He blew out a raspberry of tween irritation. "I'm not stupid. I stayed far away."

Not far enough. Someone following her and taking pot shots, she could handle. But they needed to stay away from her son. This made three incidents.

Three.

Threatening her baby.

Like fuck.

Once Nico went to bed, she once again logged into KM and put in a call to Mother.

She told her handler of her latest odd incident.

"I don't like it," Mother mused aloud. "Too many coincidences for my liking. I'll have you moved tonight."

It was tempting.

However, at the same time, Carla didn't want to yank Nico out of his life. He wouldn't understand, and she couldn't make him comprehend without divulging things a young boy wasn't ready for.

"Could be that I'm overreacting." She wasn't. She also didn't like the idea of some asshole running her out of town.

"And if you're not?"

Carla sighed. "I don't know what to do. On the one

hand, if this is just a shitty week, then I'm uprooting Nico for nothing. The only way I can be sure is to watch him twenty-four-seven, which isn't feasible. He will wonder why he's not going to school, and I'm staying home from work."

"Holing yourself up in your house is not a solution. I think you should go away for a few days."

"How does that help?"

"It gets you out of sight."

"What if they follow?"

"If they follow, then we'll have to take more drastic action." In other words, put a bullet in someone's head.

"And if they don't?"

"Then you enjoy yourself for a few days. And when you come back, if it continues, we act."

"Do I really need to run?" The idea ran counter to her gut, which wanted her to shoot something. "So far, I've only seen them in connection with the school." First night at the soccer field, then following her from it, and now, trying to steal Nico from the sidewalk in front.

"Which means, it could just be a crime based on location. They saw you, or Nico, and decided to act. The question still remains: why?"

"Because they're assholes," was Carla's smartass reply.

"Assholes or not, we need to be prepared. The next attack might hit closer to home."

"They've yet to make an appearance on my street."

"If they've been tracking you via your presence at the school, could be they don't know where you live. However, it's only a matter of time before they figure it out. Someone will blab if asked."

"Which means, they might hit my place next."

"They might, but you won't be there," Mother stated. "I'll have someone watching your house, office, and Nico's school while you're gone. See if someone is stalking you."

Probably Aunt Judy, who wouldn't look amiss popping in and out of Carla's house to water plants and bring in the mail.

"Leaving for a few days means Nico will have to miss school. How will I explain it?"

"You don't have to. You're his mother."

True. But Carla worked hard to maintain her cover of ordinary mom. One who was broke. Single moms working paycheck to paycheck didn't go on vacation out of the blue. Unless... "I think I know where I can go for a few days."

She hung up with Mother, removed the signal-jamming device, and then—in case anyone watched—pretended to browse online for a bit. She did a search on the Yaguara Academy. Went through their website. Perused photos. Then did some online searches for Pasadena, the city it was based in. Once she'd done her due diligence, she finally dialed his number.

When Moore picked up and said a deep "Hello,"

her tummy fluttered, and she sounded a tad breathless as she said, "I've been thinking about what you said."

"And?"

"Get him that invite to check out the academy."

"When?"

"The sooner, the better. Before I change my mind."

"Our next soccer practice has been cancelled due to the city putting some pesticide on the field. So, how's tomorrow?"

Even sooner than expected, which was perfect. "Meet me at my place, and I'll follow you." They set a time, and she hung up.

Carla took a deep breath. *Let's see if trouble follows me out of town.*

And if it did...then the gun she planned to pack would come in handy.

CHAPTER SEVEN

ARRIVING AT CARLA'S PLACE, Philip found her outside cursing up a storm. It involved a mixture of English swear words and some Spanish ones. Pacing back and forth by her minivan, she was the epitome of an angry Latina, but with good reason.

Her newly fixed van was sitting on four flat tires.

When Philip exited his car, she whirled and took some of her rage out on him. Good thing he had shoulders broad enough to handle it.

"Look at what some motherfucking asshole did to my van! What the fuck is wrong with people?"

"They didn't get hugged enough as a child?" Philip offered, which earned him a glare.

"I never even heard them doing it," she hissed, seeming very offended. "And with the downpour we had overnight, my camera didn't catch shit."

"Even if you recognized the guys who did this,

what could you do? Tire slashing is a petty crime. The cops won't even bother booking them."

"Do?" Her brow arched, and her smile turned wicked. "I'll tell you what I'd do. Hunt their little bitch-assses down and hurt them until they cried for their mommies, that's what I'd do." Carla tossed her hair and ended with a *humph* sound.

There was probably something severely wrong with Philip because rather than be horrified by her words, he was strangely turned on by her feisty courage.

He waved a hand at her abused van. "I guess this means you want to cancel the trip."

"Like hell," she snarled. "Nico is still going on this trip, but it might take a few hours. I've put in a call to a guy who does onsite tire repair. Which will cost an arm and a leg. Motherfucking asshole!" She flung her hands into the air and stomped.

"Or you could just ride with me." The suggestion made sense, so why did she turn such a surprised gaze on him?

"Ride with you? I don't think that's a good idea."

"Why not? Using one vehicle will save on gas." He appealed to her frugal side.

"I am already imposing enough by accepting your offer."

"It's not imposing since we're going to the same place."

"I'd rather wait for my van." She stubbornly shook her head.

Nico, who'd been sitting quietly on the step this entire time came to Philip's rescue. "We should ride with Coach, Mami. You're too angry to drive."

"Am not," she huffed.

Nico arched a brow. "You used the f-word twenty-three times since you came outside."

"Okay, maybe I'm a little mad. But I have a reason to be pissed."

"You do," Philip agreed. "However, you're letting the little dipshits win."

"They won when they destroyed my savings with this stunt." She waved a hand at the flat rubber.

"Won't your insurance cover it?"

She glared. "Only an idiot makes a useless claim."

He blinked. "How is this useless? This is vandalism, which insurance covers."

"It does, but if I claim it, I will pay three to four times the cost in increased premiums for the next few years. And, before you argue, I know this for a fact. I work for them."

"Oh. Don't you get a discount?"

"No." She pursed her lips and glared a little more at her van. Softened her gaze when she glanced over at her son and finally sighed. "Fine. I'll go with you, but only if we take turns driving."

She stalked off, and he held in a laugh as her son mouthed, "Don't let her, Coach." Then the boy widened his eyes and whispered, "She's scary behind the wheel."

"I heard that!" she hollered. To which, Nico laughed.

The boy had a good attitude about him, which he'd obviously learned from his mom. Or so Philip assumed. Philip had yet to see anything but her prickly side. Then again, he'd mostly seen her under duress thus far. It made him wonder what she was really like when she relaxed and wasn't being shot at or victimized.

She emerged from the house with a suitcase and a large purse.

"Can I grab that for you?" he politely offered. He didn't expect her to say yes, so he was caught off guard by the case being thrust in his direction.

His arms sagged at the weight. "What did you pack? The kitchen sink?"

"Gun collection," she said with a flat expression.

He laughed as he swung the suitcase into the trunk of his car.

"Careful," she said. "Might set off the hand grenades." She turned to Nico. "Put your stuff in the trunk, please." The boy grabbed two knapsacks: one with his soccer gear, and the other, Philip assumed, filled with clothes. Nico packed lighter than his mom.

"We ready?" Philip asked.

"Almost," Carla grumbled. "Let me just grab my laptop and lock up."

Moments later, they were on the road, and not much was said as she tapped on her phone.

It was Nico who broke the stale silence. "Mami says I'm going to try out for the Yaguara Academy team."

"You are."

"Yay." Nico beamed from his spot between the two front seats. "I've been following their best player, Kole. He just graduated and got drafted to Spain."

"Negotiated a sweet contract, too," Philip added.

"I want to be a soccer star when I grow up."

"You already are, *mijito*," Carla replied, finally looking away from her phone.

"I'm good, but I'm not as good as Kole. Yet," Nico added.

"How did you get a tryout for Nico so quickly?" she asked.

"I happen to know the owner of the academy." Understatement, but revealing more might see her demanding that he stop the car. He wouldn't put it past her.

"You know Mr. Oliveira?" Nico's awe was plain to hear.

"I do."

Carla craned in her seat to glance at her son. "How do you know his name?"

"Because everyone knows about the academy." Said in a *duh* tone of voice. "I read all about him. He had a son who was like this super soccer player until he died."

"How sad," Carla said by rote.

Philip took over the history lesson. "After Santos's death, Mr. Oliveira started a foundation in his son's memory. The Yaguara Academy and other schools around the world are the result."

"He makes soccer stars," Nico exclaimed.

"Not just stars," Philip interjected. "He gives kids a chance to live up to their full potential. For some, it ends up meaning a contract in the big leagues. For others, a good education to give them a good start in life."

"You make him sound like a philanthropist," Carla said with a curled lip.

"Because he is.

Carla snorted. "More like the tax breaks are really worth his while."

"Think what you like. You'll probably end up meeting him, and then you can see for yourself."

And maybe Philip would figure out why Oliveira had hired him to convince Carla to bring her son out for a visit. He just hoped Carla never found out about his ulterior motive in coaching her son's team. She didn't seem like the forgiving type.

They stopped for lunch on the road, with Carla insisting on a window seat. She spent more time staring out the dirty glass that overlooked the busy parking lot than chatting. Philip and Nico managed to keep the conversation flowing, but when the boy left to use the washroom, Philip prodded Carla.

"Is something wrong? You keep staring out that window like you're expecting someone to show up."

She turned a dark gaze on Philip. "Not expecting anyone. Just people watching."

"You look more like you're plotting murder."

At the statement, her lips quirked. "And if I am?"

"Seems kind of public for it."

"Which is why you lure them to a spot out of sight."

"Lure them how? Got some cookies hidden in your giant purse?"

"No treats. Guess I'll have to rely on my feminine charms." Her lips quirked.

At that, he snorted. "What charm?" He realized what he'd said too late, but she didn't take offense.

"I can be nice when I like."

"And how often does that happen?" Philip teased.

Carla uttered a small laugh. "Not much, I'll give you that. Most people disappoint me."

"And then you plot their murder?"

"If the price is right." She met his riposte with quick wit.

"These people you murder, what did they do to deserve it?"

Carla leaned back in her seat and crossed her arms. "Does it matter if they're guilty of a crime?"

"I think killing should always serve a purpose." Having a deeper meaning helped with the guilt.

"Not always. I murder spiders in the house because I won't suffer one to live."

"You *should* kill spiders in your house. Only way to prevent them from crawling in your mouth when you sleep."

She coughed and gagged. "Gross. No. Ew." She closed her eyes and shook her head. "You did not just say that."

"It's a proven fact."

"Know any other facts?" she asked, her expression glinting with humor.

"I know that you're nervous about what happened to your van."

"Starting to think the damned thing is cursed," she grumbled. "First the windows, now the tires."

"The way Fergus talked... Is vandalism not common?"

"I wouldn't say it doesn't happen, but usually not so close together."

"Could someone be targeting you?" he asked offhandedly.

"Yes. No. Maybe." She shrugged. "Do people really need much of a reason to commit a crime these days?"

"Could be someone pissed at you. Client. Someone you cut off in traffic. A person you might have shut out of your life."

She snorted. "It's not some ex-boyfriend if that's what you're hinting at. I already told you, I don't date."

"At all?"

"There a reason why you're asking?"

Yeah, because he was mighty fascinated by her.

"You're—" The words he might have foolishly spilled remained unspoken as Nico returned, eyes wide as he claimed, "They have a urinal that is like twenty feet long to pee in."

"You better have washed your hands," Carla admonished.

"I did."

"Do I have to kill anyone for bothering you?" she asked.

"No, Mami." Said with the eye-rolling disdain that only a tween could manage.

"We should get going. We still have quite a few hours of driving," Carla remarked.

As they paid for their meal—with Carla insisting on covering her and Nico's portions—Philip found himself thinking about their conversation. About the other side of Carla he'd briefly seen.

There was a woman of humor inside the tough shell. The sarcasm might be too much for some, but he found it a refreshing change from the women he'd met who simpered and pretended frailty. Not his type at all. He wanted an equal. A partner.

A lover...

Despite Carla's claim that she wasn't interested in

dating, Philip couldn't stop thinking about her. Lusting after her, and wondering how she'd taste.

However, he doubted anything would come of his desire. Especially once he read the next text from his boss.

No hotel. Bring them to me.

Philip tried to argue. *I doubt she'll agree.*

The reply? *Make it happen.*

CHAPTER EIGHT

"FUCKING HELL." By the time seven o'clock hit, Carla was cranky from too many hours in the car. A mood that didn't improve as they discovered that not a single hotel or motel had rooms for rent.

Not. One.

Some conference that drew tens of thousands of people had come to town.

Philip had already apologized a dozen times. "Sorry. I didn't know that was happening this week."

Just her luck. "I guess we'll have to drive to the next town over to find a place."

"It's late."

"And? We can't exactly sleep in the car," she snapped, showing her irritation even if she was more annoyed with herself. She should have booked a room ahead of time. Never should have come.

"I have a better idea," Philip stated. "We can stay at—"

She stopped him before he could say it. "I am not couch surfing at some stranger's house."

"First off, no couch. You'd get a bed. And Mr. Oliveira is not entirely a stranger."

She leaned her head back and groaned. "You want to ask the owner of the academy a favor? How is that supposed to be a good thing?"

"Because he would be pissed if I didn't offer. The guy is loaded with a house big enough for a dozen people to sleep and not get in each other's way. It's not a big deal. He hosts people all the time."

"I told you, I don't do charity."

"Stop being so damned prickly. This isn't charity. You seem to forget, Mr. Oliveira wants Nico to play for him."

She snorted. "He's never even seen him in action."

"Don't kid yourself. Oliveira knew about Nico before I even told him."

"How?"

"The man knows his athletics. He's been hand-picking students for the academy for years, finding rising talent and then cultivating it. He watches videos all the time of games from teams all across the country."

"So he preys on children."

"Hardly."

"Then what does he get out of it?"

He shrugged. "You'll have to ask him."

Lips pressed into a flat line, Carla looked out the window and didn't speak for a few minutes.

Nico leaned between the seats. "I'm hungry, and I have to go."

Carla sighed. "Fine. Call Oliveira. Ask if we can spend one night. Just one," she admonished. "We will find somewhere else tomorrow."

She regretted her choice the moment they drove through the gates, manned by a guard. While Nico smooshed his face to the glass and "oohed," she noted the opulence of the grounds. Perfectly tended shrubs. An interlocked stone driveway that went on for at least half a mile. A roundabout in front of the mansion with a massive fountain.

A water feature almost big enough to swim in.

More cameras. Carla noted them strategically placed and would wager they had motion sensors. Kind of a positive thing given she still wondered if the problems plaguing her at home would follow. If they did, there should at least be a warning.

The house itself was bigger than many a motel she'd occupied—about three stories—and wide. The banks of windows would take an army of squeegee folks to clean. Only a few showed shining lights. She wondered how fast the electrical meter spun when everything was turned on. She was the cheap mother who put her Christmas lights on a two-hour timer. Lit just long enough to make her child smile, then off to keep the bill from climbing into digits that made her wince.

Having money offshore didn't mean she was frivolous. She could pinch a penny with the best of them, which was why she frowned at the opulence she saw. So many wasted dollars in vases with perfectly cultivated flowers spilling from them, lining a stone slab path leading to the massive front door. Tall enough for a giant and made of carved wood. She could probably pay off her mortgage with what those cost.

Even though the car was parked, she continued to stare and wonder what the fuck they were doing here. This wasn't the kind of place Carla ever stepped foot into. Or if she did, it was through the back door with the servants.

She sat long enough that Philip made it around the car and opened her door like a gentleman. Problem being, Carla wasn't a lady.

She grabbed for the handle, meaning to pull it shut.

He held on and kept it ajar. "What are you doing?"

"We can't stay here." The very idea of setting foot in the mansion filled her with an inexplicable panic.

"Why not?"

"Have you seen this place?" She waved a hand. "It's way too fancy."

"And?"

"I'm not," she snapped. Carla was a girl most at home in worn jeans and T-shirts with rude sayings in a house that looked lived in. This place screamed, "*don't touch.*"

"You don't have to be fancy to enjoy someone's hospitality."

She gave him a side-eye. "Do you have a smartass answer for everything?"

A grin pulled his lips. "Yes. Are you going to keep arguing?"

"Probably." Because she really didn't want to be here. She felt out of her element, and it wasn't just about the house. Philip, the nearness of him, had something to do with it, as well.

He leaned down and murmured, "Don't be a pussy."

Had he said anything else, she would have left. Calling her bravery into question, though?

"I'm not a fucking coward. I just don't think we should be staying here."

"Well, you don't get a choice. My butt is killing me, I am starving, and you're being a baby."

Her mouth snapped shut, especially since Nico was snickering.

Philip arched a brow. "Well?"

"I think you suck." A childish retort that had Nico outright laughing as Carla exited the car.

The front door opened, and a slim fellow emerged wearing dark gray slacks and a lighter gray shirt and vest. He came at them fast. Her hand dropped into her purse, curling around the grip of her pistol.

However, the guy didn't have any eyes for her. He snapped a jaunty, "Hello, Mr. Moore. Let me grab your bags."

A bell boy? How fucking rich was this dude?

The spry guy grabbed two cases and sprinted into the house. She frowned and hugged her laptop case close but relaxed the hand in the purse.

While she kept a wary eye on everything, Nico babbled at Philip, not daunted at all. He even managed an enthusiastic "hello" when they reached the door, and an honest-to-goodness butler stood just inside.

In a suit. The kind that had a coat with tails.

Utterly ridiculous and yet, at the same time, having all kinds of visible staff gave the house the feel of a hotel—which strangely relaxed Carla. If the guy paid people to work this late into the evening, then he wouldn't care about a few extra people dirtying some linens and eating his food.

One only hoped the food provided would be the normal kind and not some weird, fancy crap like caviar and that liver spread stuff.

"Evening, madame, young sir. Mr. Moore, always a pleasure."

"Hey, Owen, I want you to meet Carla and her son, Nico. They're in town a few days while they check out the academy."

"Mr. Oliveira already informed me of our guests. Unfortunately, he is not here at the moment, as he is away conducting business, but he left instructions to make yourselves comfortable. If you need anything, please let me know."

"This is a nice house," Nico remarked.

"It is, young sir. We have available for your entertainment, a billiards room, an intimate movie theatre, a bowling alley, an outdoor heated pool, and a stable if you enjoy riding."

"That's insane," Carla muttered.

The butler offered her a snooty rebuttal. "Given Mr. Oliveira's preference for privacy, it enables him to enjoy some of his favorite pastimes in an intimate social setting. We also have a sauna and hot tub on the rooftop of the west wing, as well as a fully equipped gym."

"What about a resort map?" Carla quipped.

"We offer an app with directions and a list of the rooms."

"You're kidding, right?" she blurted.

The butler's face maintained its stoic appearance as he replied. "We did it to save the trees."

Philip stepped in. "You won't get lost, and if you do, there are intercoms in each room. Hit the star button, and someone will help you find your way."

"If you'll follow me, I will show you to your rooms and have refreshments brought." Owen led the way with Nico keeping pace at his side going up the grand staircase.

"Coming?" Philip asked, his foot on the first step.

Carla almost said no. But that would come across

as childish and petty. She'd been given a chance to stay in luxury at no cost to her. No cost that she knew of, which bothered her. In her experience, people always wanted something.

Nico was almost to the top while she hesitated. Since he was about to move out of sight, she had to make a choice. She swept past Philip. "I swear, if they try and feed me snails, I'll hurt you."

"No snails," he promised, following her. "But there might be grasshoppers."

She stopped and whirled. "You'd better be joking."

"They're a great source of protein." He moved past her. "Don't worry, you won't even taste them."

"No, seriously, tell me there are no bugs in the food."

Having reached the top of the stairs, he paused to give her a grin. "Don't tell me you're too chicken to try something new?"

She stomped up the remainder of the steps. "You are not funny."

"Says you. I am highly entertained right now. Because you're not as fierce as you appear, Carla Baker."

"Being scared of bugs isn't a weakness. They're dangerous."

A claim that caused him to snort.

"Don't laugh. A single tick can paralyze."

"Might as well hide inside and wear armor." He

rolled his eyes before walking in the direction Nico had gone. She could see her son halfway up a long hall.

She hastened her steps. "Keep bugging me, Moore. I'll shove you over the railing and claim it was an accident."

He looked over the edge. "It's only about twenty feet. I'd survive."

"Are you telling me to revise my plan to kill you?"

"You'd kill me for teasing?" He cast her a smile.

"I also murder people for putting paper in the plastic recycling bin."

"Then I'll do my best to avoid that."

The butler had stopped in front of a door and opened it. Nico disappeared from sight, and her anxiety heightened, but she didn't act. Moore appeared more than relaxed, and while she did hear squealing, it was from Nico's excitement. She soon understood why.

The room she was assigned proved nicer than a hotel. Nicer than any place she'd ever stayed in, as a matter of fact. Most of her special jobs were undercover, which meant she stuck to places that didn't have the money for cameras and hired staff that didn't ask questions.

While she remained wary—and wondered when the other shoe would drop—Nico was in his glory, squealing at the size of the television in his room, conveniently equipped with a game system. He had his own bathroom with a giant, jetted tub. Even a snack bar with a mini-fridge stocked with juice and water, plus a cabinet full of snacks.

Her room was right across the hall, done in a white and rose gold theme. Fit for a princess. Little did anyone know she'd packed her set of knives and not a tiara.

Moore didn't stick around, and she restrained an urge to peek her head out the door to see where he ended up.

She didn't care.

Curiosity wasn't at all why she crossed the hallway to Nico's room, and she only looked left and right out of habit. For protection, not to spot that Moore was in the room at the far end of the hall.

Entering Nico's room, she found him bouncing on the bed. "Nico. Don't do that."

He stilled and rolled over with a wide grin. "This place is awesome, Mami."

"Don't get too comfy. And take off your shoes!" she exclaimed.

Given the place felt like a hotel, and both Owen and Philip kept theirs on, she'd never even thought to slip off her own footwear.

Nico gave her running shoes a pointed look.

She shook her finger at him. "Don't start." She kicked them off. "We are guests here."

"Guests, yes, but do get comfortable." Philip appeared in the doorway. "Owen is grabbing you some food."

"You eating with us, Coach?" Nico asked. "I can sit on the bed." The room only held a pair of chairs in front of the television.

Before Carla could uninvite Philip, he shook his head. "Sorry, bud. I've got a few things I need to take care of. See you in the morning."

He was leaving?

She rose and moved quickly to the door as Philip waved.

She exited and hissed, "You can't dump us here and run."

"I am not dumping nor running."

"Where are you going?"

"To see a few friends."

His reminder made her wonder who he was going to see. A girlfriend, perhaps? Not that she cared. She totally lied to herself in the hopes it would stop her from seeing red. "Have fun."

"Doubtful. I'd rather hang out here with you guys and unwind. It's been a long day, and it's late. I'm sure after your snack, you'll want to hit the sack early."

Probably. Still, how dare he use logic? "See you in the morning." She shut the door in a huff. She couldn't truly explain her anger.

The butler made it clear that they were welcome, so she didn't need Moore, yet she noticed his absence as she ate with Nico.

Especially since the chicken nuggets, potato

wedges, and slices of fresh fruit didn't have any bugs at all. And the ketchup was Heinz.

Right after Nico finished eating, his eyes drooped. It was approaching nine o'clock, and Carla put him to bed before returning to her room.

Where she paced.

Bored. Restless.

Her mind kept straying to Moore. Wondering what he was doing. Had he finished his business? Was he in his room?

She could knock and see.

But what would she say if he opened the door? She didn't have a plausible excuse for bothering him. Because she certainly wouldn't admit she missed his presence. Miss a stranger? As if.

Then again, he wasn't really a stranger anymore. They'd not talked much to each other at any rate. All her knowledge of him was secondhand since Philip didn't mind conversing with Nico when he put his tablet down and got excited about the scenery they passed.

The guys even got into a discussion about sports. Their back-and-forth banter wasn't something she'd ever seen her son indulge in before with another person. The weird part was that seeing them bond didn't rouse her jealousy, but rather a certain nostalgia. It showed a preview of what Nico had missed out on by not having a father in his life.

He doesn't need a father, he has me. Not to

mention, if she shopped for a daddy, Moore wouldn't fit the bill. He was much too good-looking for one. Probably a ladies' man.

He also appeared reasonably intelligent and well-spoken. He might even be the type who preferred long-term relationships. All of which made him sound too good to be true. Would that kind of man seriously be single?

Philip claimed he was.

Did she believe it? Did it even matter? She wasn't interested in him. Not one bit.

She peeked out the window of her room. She had a view of the garden and the pool, the blue length of it massive and lit with underwater lights.

A pity she'd not brought a suit. A swim might have burned off some of her excess agitation. The energy needed an outlet, and her room, while large, wasn't big enough.

Despite her warning to Nico to not go wandering, she exited her room and went prowling. Probably not the politest thing she could do. However, she yearned to know a little bit more about the situation. Because there was something odd going on.

It started with the fact that all the hotels Moore stopped at were full. As in not a single room available. Which wasn't completely unheard of, and yet, at the same time, cancellations happened all the time. What were the chances that the six hotels he tried didn't have a single bed available?

She would try again in the morning to locate new accommodations because she didn't feel right staying here. Carla wasn't one to accept charity, and this felt awfully close. Not to mention the discomfort of being surrounded by furniture and knickknacks that probably cost more than she made in a month. The silence of the house only served to increase her agitation.

The long hallway was softly lit, and she traced her path back to the stairs. She half expected to see Owen waiting at the bottom, ready to pounce and ask her if she required his services.

How convenient the way Moore had managed to get them accommodations at the house belonging to the owner of the academy. In some respects, it made sense. Moore was friends with the guy, after all. Hence the invite for Nico to try out. But on the other hand, how chummy were they? Because she didn't buy Philip's bullshit story of Oliveira being a benevolent host. This house oozed wealth. The kind that wasn't meant for rambunctious boys and their mothers. Moore's claim that Oliveira wanted to woo Nico to become one of his students didn't ring true either. Why would this rich man go out of his way to impress a student who couldn't afford his academy? Surely, he had more applicants than he could handle.

Carla had to find out more.

She held her finger down on the power button of her phone for seventeen seconds, then dialed a special number, which put the device into scramble mode.

Even if someone tried, they wouldn't be able to decipher the signal. To make things more difficult, she headed outside via the terrace door she'd seen in the massive living room—and by massive, she meant super high ceiling and the size of a basketball court, with a half-dozen couches and even more chairs scattered throughout.

The phone was answered within two rings. "There's my sweet girl. How did your trip go?" Mother asked.

"Not so good. We should have made a reservation. There wasn't a hotel room to be found."

"Oh, dear. Where are you now then?"

"Staying at the house of the guy who owns the Yaguara Academy."

"Really?" Mother's voice dropped a level. "How generous of him."

"Isn't it, though?" Carla didn't bother to hide her wry reply. "Coach Moore has painted him to be some kind of philanthropist."

"Must be, given the interest he takes in undeveloped talent."

They kept their conversation couched in case of listeners, but Carla knew that Mother was already digging up everything she could on Oliveira. Something Carla should have done before leaving on this trip; however, she'd not imagined they'd get so close to the owner of the academy. A mistake rectified because, in her profession, it sometimes paid to be suspicious.

"Place is nice. Huuuuge," Carla said, exaggerating the word. "I might have to GPS Nico to keep track of him."

"How long will you be staying?" asked Mother.

"One night. I'm going to find us another spot to stay tomorrow."

"When does Nico try out?"

"Tomorrow afternoon. Apparently, the boys run on a special schedule to allow them early dismissal so they can have afternoon practices."

"Leaving them the evenings for homework and relaxation. That is a nice perk."

"I guess." Carla had never known relaxation. Growing up, with her dad out of the picture, her mother worked twice as hard to make ends meet, which meant the kids had to do their part. As soon as they were old enough, they got a job to contribute. Homework rarely got done. That explained her grades.

"How is the handsome coach?"

Carla almost blushed, especially since she'd never told Mother that Moore was anything of the sort. Which meant Mother had already been digging into him. "He's fine."

"Just fine? I think you should get to know him better." Code-speak for the fact that Mother was having trouble finding any dirt. "I sent Aunt Judy over to keep an eye on your house," Mother remarked, changing the subject.

More code, indicating she'd put a KM operative on

the case. If there were something amiss, Aunt Judy would ferret it out.

"While she's there, see if she can get something done about my van."

"Already taken care of. Damned teenagers," Mother exclaimed. "Now, I know you don't want to hear this, but I think it's time you move to a nicer neighborhood."

Carla sighed. "I'd rather not, but given all that's happened, I guess I'd better start thinking about it." In other words, it might be time to relocate.

"Perhaps this academy thing is just what you and Nico need. A new city, fresh start."

Given Nico seemed excited, it could be a good plan. At least she wouldn't need to give him a weak excuse as to why he needed to leave everything he knew. "I guess it depends on how well he does at the tryout. I should go. I'll call you tomorrow." Carla hung up, not allowing Mother to respond, and slowly turned, fixing Moore with a stare. "Eavesdrop often?" She'd only barely caught the sound of a shoe scuffing garden stone. Good thing she hadn't said anything she shouldn't have. She'd hate to have to kill Philip. A feat that would be difficult, given the number of cameras around.

"I didn't want to interrupt." He came closer, hands shoved into his pockets, which made her twitch. Did he have a gun or knife hidden in there?

She had a piece tucked under her arm inside her sweater. Pulling it seemed premature, though.

"I was talking to Mo—my mother." She almost forgot the *my*, which would have sounded odd.

"I couldn't help but overhear you discussing big life changes."

"You mean the part about me moving?" Her nose wrinkled. "Yeah. Maybe. If the neighborhood's gone to shit, then I don't want Nico getting hurt by accident."

"The timing might be perfect if everything goes well at tryouts."

"Assuming we want to make the jump to Pasadena."

"It's a nice city."

"How would you know?"

"Have you forgotten? I'm from here."

"If it's so nice, why leave?"

"I didn't, technically. The coaching job is tempo-rary. I'm doing it as a favor."

"Hold on, if it's temporary, then that means you have a place here."

"I do."

"Then why aren't you staying at your house?" she asked, suspicion furrowing her brow.

"Since I was supposed to be gone for a few weeks, I am having the whole place repainted."

"Oh." She tucked her phone in her pocket, suddenly at a loss for words. Which wasn't like her. She was the brash one with a smartass reply for everything. Yet there was something about Moore, an appeal that she couldn't explain. He seemed so darned cultured. Respectable.

Handsome in his button-down shirt.

Mother needs to dig deeper. Find out what is wrong with him. He'd be easier to dislike then.

"Why are you out here?" she asked. It seemed kind of fishy that they'd both gone for a walk at the same time.

"I saw you from my bedroom window."

The fact that he spied should have angered Carla. Instead, a strange warmth filled her. "You followed me?"

"I did. I wanted to make sure you were doing okay."

She arched a brow. "Why do you care how I feel?"

"If you're stressed, then Nico will sense it. It could affect his playing abilities."

A snort escaped her. "I am always stressed."

"Why?"

"I'm a single mother living paycheck to paycheck." Who spent a lot of time worrying about her son. A son who kept reminding her that he wasn't a baby. The older Nico got, the less he needed her, and the more alone she felt.

"Sounds hard."

"Lonely." The word escaped her before she could stop it.

Moore stepped closer, and she didn't move away,

even though he invaded her space. This close, she was forced to tilt her head to maintain eye contact. She felt electricity in the air, snapping between them. Breathless anticipation.

Her heart raced, and she, who was never nervous, had butterflies.

"I lied. I didn't come out here because of Nico." Moore lifted a hand and brushed a loose strand of hair behind her ear. "I noticed you wandering and had to come see you."

"Why?" The word escaped on a whisper.

"Because I wanted to do this." He leaned in and kissed her. His mouth slowly caressed hers, a cautious exploration.

She could have shoved him away. Slapped him. Bitten his lip.

However, his touch ignited something within her. A flame started low in her belly, and it tingled. Warmed. Made her yearn for more.

She grabbed the back of his neck and drew him closer, deepened the kiss, caught his lower lip for a suck, letting her tongue slip between for a taste.

He made a sound—half-groan, half-sigh—and chased her tongue back, sucking on it. His arms came around her, his hands on her waist, pulling her closer to him, close enough that the rigidness of his erection pressed against her lower belly. His hand skimmed upward, tracing the lower edges of her ribs—

Reality slammed into her. If he kept touching, he'd

find her gun. He'd ask questions. She'd find out how deep the koi pond was.

She pulled away. "We shouldn't do this." A lie that ignored the fact that her lips tingled, her sex throbbed, and she wanted nothing more than to sit him on the stone bench and straddle him. She did none of the above. She stepped around him and headed to the house, expecting he'd act at any moment. Grab her. Demand more.

Instead, he chose to murmur, "I know we shouldn't. I just can't help myself."

CHAPTER NINE

HANDS IN HIS POCKETS, Philip watched Carla walk into the house, a habit he'd fallen into. A nice view each time.

He'd probably lose his man card for admitting it, but damn if he didn't feel tingles when she was around. As for the kiss they shared? Explosive. At least for him. She, on the other hand, didn't seem as affected given she'd left.

Probably for the best. Getting involved wasn't the brightest thing he could do.

So why had it happened? He should have stayed inside, yet something had possessed him to track her down when he spotted her from a window. An urge—no, a need—to talk to her. Be with her.

When he found her, he heard her on the phone and shadowed her steps, waiting for her to finish. He'd caught some of her conversation and saw her shoulders slump as she'd discussed moving. Obviously, not an option that pleased.

Defeat wasn't a good look on her. It made Philip want to make promises that he couldn't be sure he could keep. Made him want to tell her not to worry because it would turn out all right. A dumb thing to vow since he couldn't be certain of that.

Seeing those slashed tires on her van had made him wonder if something sinister was afoot. First the drive-by incident, and then the vandalism. Maybe someone had it out for her.

Was that why she'd called him out of the blue and said "yes" to his offer of getting Nico an invite for tryouts? A trip out of town provided a convenient escape.

It sure took Mr. Oliveira by surprise when Philip had called him to mention the news.

"She agreed to bring him for a tryout. We'll be arriving late-afternoon. I booked a room at the Hilton for them."

"Cancel it. I want you to bring them here," his boss had ordered.

"I can't do that. She'll refuse."

"Then convince her."

"How am I supposed to do that?"

In the end, it had proven easier than expected. Philip had walked in and out of a few hotels, claiming they were booked solid. Luckily, Carla hadn't caught on that he lied.

Still, he had to wonder if he'd done the right thing. When he'd taken the job, Oliveira had made it sound simple.

"I need you to do something for me. I'm interested in a specific boy for the academy."

"Then why not send him an offer?"

"I don't think the mother will agree."

"Then send Kyle to convince her." Kyle being the main coach at the academy.

"I can't spare him, not with finals coming up."

Hence how Philip had ended up taking over for Coach Mathews—who'd been more than happy to leave once a higher-paying position opened up near his girlfriend. Philip had expected it to take longer to convince Carla. The incidents played in his favor, which made him wonder...

Surely, Oliveira wasn't involved in her recent issues.

He stared at the house. The massive mansion owned by a man who didn't let much get in his way. Even a little thing like morals.

After all, look at what he had Philip doing for him. Security was only part of his job. The other part would land him in jail if he ever got caught.

Coaching and convincing a woman to bring her son to Oliveira, though? That was new. Strange. Concerning even.

It was too late now to wonder what his boss really wanted with Nico. Also too late for Philip to come clean with Carla. She probably wouldn't react well to finding out that he'd lied to her about Oliveira and everything.

She was right. They shouldn't be kissing.

Even if it had been a most excellent kiss.

CHAPTER TEN

CARLA WOKE the moment her door opened, then relaxed, easing her fingers away from the gun hidden under her pillow. Nico bounced in with a grin a mile-wide.

"Wakey, wakey, Mami!" he crooned.

She feigned a grumpy mien. "Wake? Are you insane? It's the crack of dawn. An ungodly hour."

"It's almost seven o'clock." Which, in a child's mind, was plenty late.

"What's the rush?"

"I wanna check this place out."

The curiosity brimming in her son didn't mean she allowed free rein. Carla sat up in bed. "This isn't a place for us to go running around in."

"Then I'll walk." Spoken with the stubborn insistence of a child.

"How about we don't go poking our noses anywhere we shouldn't."

Nico's lips turned down. "I wasn't going to break nothing."

"I know, *mijito*, but until we meet our host, we need to be good guests. Not everyone wants sticky fingers touching their things."

"My hands aren't sticky!" Nico exclaimed, holding them up for inspection.

Carla held in a sigh and was saved from replying by an interruption.

"Don't worry about the boy." Moore appeared behind Nico, already dressed, hair brushed. How dare he look so impeccable when she'd spent part of the night tossing and turning. For more reasons than her current problems. The man had wormed his way into her thoughts and affected her body. A body that craved something more than sleep.

Her irritation showed in her response. "I will worry because I don't need to get a bill for something that costs more than I make in a month."

"Mr. Oliveira wouldn't charge you. So stop worrying. Besides, Nico is light on his feet. The whole reason we're here. He won't knock anything over, will you?"

A rapid shake of Nico's head and a hopping dance from one foot to another was her son's reply.

"Why don't you head downstairs and see if breakfast is served," Philip said. "They make the best fresh waffles with whipped cream I've ever had."

"I love whipped cream." Nico's eyes lit up, and he was gone before she could open her mouth.

Carla turned a glare on Moore. "Really? You're going to encourage sugar this early in the morning?"

"A little bit of sugar won't hurt."

"Says a guy with no kids. Sweets make kids hyper."

"He'll burn that energy off soon enough with his roaming."

"I don't want him roaming," she reiterated.

"Why not?"

Was Moore being purposely obtuse? "Because this isn't our home," she exclaimed.

"It's also not a museum. Let the boy be a boy."

"You've got an answer for everything, don't you?" she grumbled, swinging her legs over the edge of the mattress. The sleigh bed sat high off the floor, lofty enough that her short legs didn't reach. She did a hop and stretched as she landed, only realizing a moment too late that he watched, his eyes trained on the strip of skin between her T-shirt and her jersey shorts.

She was decently dressed, yet her entire body flushed with heat, her nipples hardening. Something she couldn't hide. Her arms didn't cross her chest fast enough. He noticed.

His gaze, when it met hers, smoldered. Carla couldn't help recalling the kiss. Moist heat pooled between her legs. Treacherous body.

"About last night," he said.

"It never happened."

"Oh no, you don't." He stepped farther into the room but left the door open. "Don't you dare pretend there isn't something between us."

"No need to pretend. There is nothing."

"That kiss wasn't nothing."

No, that kiss was a smoldering fire waiting to ignite. "I've had better." At her obvious lie, his brow arched.

"Is that so? I hear a challenge."

"Don't you dare kiss me again." Said with a breathlessness very unlike her.

"Or what?"

"I should get dressed and find Nico." She gave Moore a verbal nudge to get him to leave.

"The boy will be fine for a few minutes. I, on the other hand, am feeling a need to prove you wrong."

"How?" Said in a soft murmur as he stepped closer. She should move away. Yet her body betrayed her.

"I think that kiss *did* mean something." He moved close enough that she had to tilt her head. Close enough she could lift on tiptoe and nibble that firm jaw.

"I meant what I said last night. We can't get involved. You're Nico's coach."

"Only until the big game, which is days away at this point. And you're making excuses. Don't tell me you're scared to kiss me again?" Moore said with a mocking tone.

The dare was obvious. It didn't stop her from acting. She rose to the challenge and pressed her lips to his, a tingle spreading through her body. Her lips parted on a sigh as he kissed her back.

Oh, how she wanted to take the kiss one step further, but she remained in control. She shut down her desire and stepped back, uttering a husky, "Happy now? I'm not scared of kissing you." She *was* frightened by the things he made her feel. Emotions were the problem. "But I'm also not about to bang you in your friend's house."

His gaze smoldered. "Then I guess I'll wait until we're elsewhere."

"That's not what I meant," she exclaimed, even as more heat pooled between her legs.

"Maybe not, but I did. I'm going to kiss you again, Carla Baker."

"Not now, you're not. I need to get dressed and find Nico." She used her son as a shield against Moore's allure.

"I'll go wrangle him. Grab a shower, take your time..." His lips curved knowingly.

Asshole.

Pretend-hating him didn't stop the quiver between her legs.

Moore shut the door as he left, and she almost followed. Wanted to open that door and drag him back in, perhaps see if she could tempt him into taking a second shower.

The very idea made her freeze.

The last time she'd let her panties make the decisions, she'd ended up in an abusive relationship.

She'd also ended up with Nico.

It had gotten her family killed.

But Philip was nothing like Matias. The guy wore collared shirts for God's sake. He drove a sedan that still held the new car smell. He worked. And not as a drug dealer or enforcer.

Still, it was a rule of hers not to casually fuck people she might have to deal with in the future. As Nico's coach, even if temporarily, Moore fell under that heading.

But I am planning to move, and even if I don't, he's not sticking around.

She shook her head to clear it of the naughty thoughts trying to sway her. She wasn't so hard up or horny that she needed to break her own rules, *good* rules, to get laid. If she wanted some cock, she could hit a bar and get lucky in an alley within twenty minutes.

Problem being, that thought didn't appeal, so obviously she wasn't as horny as she thought. Blame it on Moore's good looks and the fact that seeing him being nice to Nico had messed with her hormones. Must be getting close to that time of the month.

A half hour later, her damp hair pulled back in a ponytail, she skipped down the stairs, gun tucked safely away in her suitcase, leaving her armed only with the knife in her ankle sheath.

The stairs were a grand affair, polished wood with black wrought iron railings, all of it gleaming, scratch-free, and large enough to handle an army of debutantes. Hitting the foyer, the floor was comprised of large tiles —marble she thought, although she could be wrong. Stone and décor weren't her fortes. Another reason she didn't work for KM Design. She would wager that whatever it was, came with a hefty price tag, as did the console table of ornate wood in the middle of the entryway, adorned with a fancy bowl of fresh flowers.

The only flowers she owned was a single plastic bloom in a flower pot that Nico had painted for Mother's Day a few years ago.

Matching arches led left and right from the foyer, living room on one side, formal dining on the other. She was relieved to see no one in that staid room. The dining table, set up to seat more than thirty people, intimidated.

Not spotting Moore or Nico, Carla started to walk down the wide hall. Halfway down the massive corridor, she heard a familiar giggle.

What mischief was Nico getting into? Given she'd raised her son to have manners, Moore had more than likely done something to make her boy smile. Philip did have a way with her son, which only improved his appeal.

Jerk. Carla didn't want to like him. She really needed to work on finding something to ruin the attraction. Maybe he scratched his balls and didn't wash his hands. Or chewed like a cow when eating.

Walking in the direction of the giggle, Carla abruptly stopped as an older man emerged from a doorway. Not much taller than her, slightly heavyset, wearing a crisp suit in a steel gray color. His tanned skin was offset by the white of his hair.

He stared at her, his dark eyes not revealing anything.

Her hand itched to grab her knife, even though the man made no menacing movement. Yet something about the way he held himself set off her danger radar.

"Who are you?" she demanded, never mind the fact that he probably had more right to be here than she did.

His thick, white brows rose. "Your host. You must be Carla Baker."

Shame at her rude query almost made her apologize, but Carla didn't give in. She held herself tall. "I am. Which means, you're Mr. Oliveira."

"Call me Luiz."

The offer appeared friendly, yet something about this man bothered Carla.

"Thank you for your hospitality. I hope to be out of your hair by the afternoon." As soon as she had a chance to go online and hunt for a hotel.

"No need to do that. I'd prefer you and the boy stay here."

"Prefer?" She arched a brow.

He tried to smooth things over. "I'd like for him to stay so I can get to know him. And you."

Know them? That was the dumbest excuse she'd ever heard. Being blunt by nature, she didn't throw any punches. "Drop the bullshit. Why are we here? What do you want with Nico?" Because this was obviously about her son.

For a moment, his expression flashed with an emotion she couldn't decipher. Regret. Anger. Then a placid mask with a hint of humor took over. "Who wouldn't want to tempt an up-and-coming soccer star? I want him to play for the academy."

"Do you offer all your potential recruits a free place to stay?"

"Would you prefer I charged you?"

"Yes," she said without thinking.

"Sorry to disappoint. There won't be a bill. As you can see, my home is more than large enough to host a child and his mother."

"A child who is curious, and at times noisy."

"Your point being?"

Her lips flattened. "I've already told him to keep his hands to himself, but you might want to set some boundaries. He'll take it more seriously if it comes from you."

"What if I don't want to set any? He's a boy. Boys are curious and daring by nature."

"Sometimes, things get broken when they're too daring."

The man shrugged. "Things can be replaced. It's important for children to explore and test boundaries. Even if, sometimes, it involves going against their parents' wishes."

She frowned. "Nico's a good boy."

"Never said he wasn't. Speaking of whom, where is he? I'd like to meet him."

The man said all the right things, and yet there was something off about his replies. About this whole situation. Until she knew more, Carla would watch him. Like a hawk. Especially around her son. "You want to meet Nico, then find the waffles and whipped cream."

"Breakfast of champions," Oliveira exclaimed. "Shall we?" He swept his arm, gesturing for her to go ahead. As if. Leaving anyone at her back, even a man as old and seemingly benevolent as *Luiz*, went against her nature.

"You know the way. I'll follow."

With a shrug, Oliveira moved with quick steps down the hall to an archway at the far end, saying over his shoulder, "They're in the breakfast room."

How many rooms did a person need for meals?

The man disappeared, and she took a moment before following, standing in the doorway, taking in the scene. The sun-dappled space was framed by floor-to-ceiling windows that let in the morning sunlight and gave a glimpse of the pool, its waters gleaming and pristine. Beyond the fencing around it, she caught peeks of the garden she'd wandered.

The room itself was a bright, sunshiny mess with yellow-and-white-striped walls and a white-stained wooden table pockmarked and scratched to look aged. Yet Carla remembered enough of her KM Design lessons to know that it was fabricated. People paid lots of money to buy things that looked old.

Matching chairs with flowered-fabric cushions ringed the table, only six this time, two of which were occupied. Nico sat grinning in front of a mostly empty plate. The giant waffle had been demolished until just a quarter remained. Moore sat across from him, his plate also containing a waffle but covered by banana slices and drenched in syrup.

"Mami!" Nico squealed. "Coach Philip has the best jokes." He turned a bright smile on Moore. "Tell her the one with the tissue."

Moore smirked. "How do you get a tissue to dance?"

Nico, jiggling in his chair, couldn't contain himself. "You put a little boogie into it," he chortled. "Mami, guess why the picture went to jail?"

"I believe it was framed," Oliveira replied.

Clapping his hands, Nico beamed. "Yes. Do you know jokes, too?"

"A few," said the old man.

Philip stood, placing his napkin on the table to make introductions. "Nico, I'd like you to meet our host, Mr. Oliveira."

"Hi!" Nico waved.

Oliveira inclined his head. "Good morning, young man. I trust you found the breakfast to your satisfaction."

"It was delicious." Nico rubbed his belly. "Have some, Mami."

"Yes, please, help yourself." Their host indicated the sideboard manned by a servant in white and gray livery.

Snaring a plate, Carla stood by the vast buffet and couldn't believe the amount of food on display. Bacon, fruit, a waffle maker standing by, juice, coffee. *So much waste*, she thought with lips pressed into a disapproving line. Having grown up poor, her belly often tight with hunger, it bothered her. Imagine how many kids could go to school on a full stomach with the food on display here?

For a moment, she entertained the idea of tossing it all into the trunk of Philip's car and driving to the nearest public school to hand it out. It probably wouldn't go over well.

"Is there nothing to your liking?" asked Oliveira when Carla stood staring so long.

"More like too much to choose from." A subtle dig. She placed bacon and roasted potatoes on her plate along with some watermelon and then filled a mug with coffee, extra sugar, and lots of cream. She sat down between Nico and Moore and, a moment later, Oliveira joined them.

He seemed rather happy, considering he was

sitting down to breakfast with strangers. Then again, not everyone was an antisocial bitch like Carla.

She studied him as he spent a few moments talking to Nico. He seemed genuinely interested in everything her son had to say.

It didn't ease her mind. Nor was she happy to find Moore staring at her.

"I'll be moving us to a hotel as soon as I find a room," she said to forestall any conversation that might lead to another kiss. Not that she thought Moore would do anything in front of Nico or Oliveira. Simple logic, and yet her heart fluttered as if he might. And she sat in anticipation, almost as if hoping he'd try.

"Nonsense," Oliveira exclaimed, apparently paying attention. "You'll stay here."

"I don't know if that's appropriate. It might seem like favoritism to have Nico under your roof. Right, Coach Moore?" She gave him a pointed look.

"It's only favoritism if Nico sucks, which he doesn't?" Moore didn't help at all by winking at her son.

"We really shouldn't impose," she said.

"It's not imposing, given my home is huge. It's nice to see a young person within its confines." Oliveira cast a glance at Nico, one with an emotion she didn't trust.

What was his game? If he were a perv, he'd be sucking the barrel of her gun if he tried anything.

"*Mijito*, you have cream all over your face. Why don't you go wash up?"

Nico's lips turned down. "But—"

Moore interjected. "Meet me in the front hall when you're done, and I'll show you the stable. There's a pony in there you might like."

Before she could say a word, Nico shot off.

"A pony?" she said dryly.

"A gentle one. He won't fall off."

She held in an urge to sigh. If she said no, she'd come off as the mean bitch. "If he gets hurt..."

"I know. You'll hurt me." Moore winked as he stood. "Don't worry. He'll be fine. I need him in good shape for the practice this afternoon."

As he left, silence descended, and Carla concentrated on her plate. Fighting the urge to run after her son.

Must act normal.

Normal for her, wasn't being a meek sheep. She raised her gaze to find Oliveira watching her. "I want it to be clear now...if you touch my son in any way I deem inappropriate, I will kill you."

"I would never harm a child," he sputtered. "The very idea is ridiculous."

"Says you. Just making it clear so there's no misunderstanding. Nico is my life, and I will protect him."

"I would never cause you or your son any harm. Merely offering him a chance to develop his mind and skills."

"The chance is appreciated, but I don't think it will happen."

"Why not?" he asked.

"Cost, for one. I don't make enough money to afford your tuition."

"What if I said the foundation will offer him sponsorship."

"I'd say what's the catch?" She distrusted the offer on principle.

"No catch. We have programs in place for gifted students like your son."

A proud mama, the flattery caused her warmth, but it didn't belay her suspicion. "I'd still have to move."

"If you are concerned about expenses, I'm sure we can come to an arrangement. And before you accuse me of giving you charity, I would expect you to reimburse the cost."

"Exactly how am I supposed to repay you? I'd be quitting my job."

Oliveira snorted. "No, you wouldn't. The insurance company you work for is a large one with many branches. You'd ask for a transfer to an office in the city."

He knew about her job? Her gaze narrowed. "Have you been spying on me?"

"I prefer to term it *informing myself*. Before we extend an invitation to a potential student, we do a thorough background check."

She froze. Her credentials would weather any kind of cursory examination. Mother didn't set them up with weak identities. Still... "What kind of problems do you expect to find with a twelve-year-old?"

"Actually, it is not the child I worry about. Sometimes, a second chance is all that's needed to turn their life and attitude around. Parents, though..." He spread his hands. "Not all of them have their children's best interests at heart."

Carla chewed on a piece of bacon before replying. "I gotta say, you talk a good game, but I'm not sure I buy it. What's in it for you?"

For a moment, she expected a line of bullshit. Instead, Oliveira's expression turned sad, and he seemed to age in that moment. "My only son died before he could have a child of his own, and I never remarried when his mother succumbed to cancer. I have all this wealth, and yet no one to shower it upon. Why not try and do a bit of good?"

"Because no one does things out of the goodness of their heart. Everyone has a motive. Even you." She stood. "Thank you for breakfast. I should check on Nico."

First, however, she grabbed her phone and sent a message to Mother.

Find out everything you can about Luiz Oliveira. Because the man was lying about something. She could feel it in her gut.

CHAPTER ELEVEN

PHILIP SAW Carla coming down the path from the house and couldn't help a smile.

To his surprise, she offered one in return. She halted close to him and faced the paddock where Nico was sitting atop a pony, who was plodding along. Although, given the expression on Nico's face, he didn't care about the speed.

"Mami!" he yelled. "Look at me. I'm riding."

"Eyes in front, *mijito*," she replied, gazing at him fondly.

"Boy is a natural. Hasn't fallen once," Philip noted.

"Then I guess you live another day."

"I wouldn't let him come to harm."

She sighed. "I know you wouldn't. Sorry."

An apology? "You're his mother. You're allowed to care."

"Yeah, but I also need to remember I can't bubble wrap him."

"He's a good boy."

"Yeah, he is, but that doesn't mean I don't worry. The world is a shitty place."

"Sometimes. However, it can also be amazing." Especially when you met someone special.

She turned and leaned on the rail, eyeing him. "How did you meet Oliveira?"

The truth wasn't something he could comfortably relay yet. At the same time, it proved hard to resist the soft query in Carla's eyes. He couldn't keep lying forever. Might as well rip off the bandage of truth now and get it over with. "Mr. Oliveira hired me years ago for a contract and thought I was competent. Rather than employ me on a case-by-case basis, he made me a generous offer to work for him full-time."

The expression on her face hardened. "So, you're telling me you're not friends. You work for him."

He nodded.

She slugged him hard enough that the air whooshed from him. "Guess I deserved that."

"You lied to me."

"Not intentionally."

"Did the words come out of your mouth?" was her sarcastic reply.

"Yes, but—"

She sliced a hand through the air. "Don't bother

giving me a bullshit answer. He sent you to my town, didn't he? Sent you to spy on my kid."

"The word is *scout*. As in talent scout. Happens all the time."

"Scouts don't pretend to be coaches and then cozy up to a single mother in order to con her into travelling hours from home."

"He wanted me to check out Nico in person." Which was admittedly odd. But since it seemed easy enough, Philip agreed.

"And one practice was all it took?" she sneered. "Seems like an awful lot of trouble to go to. Why not just be honest from the beginning and say that you were there looking for talent?"

"Because you said it yourself. Most parents think their child is special. I don't need to fend off a dozen parents when I'm only interested in one particular woman."

Her eyes flashed. "Is that what the kiss was about? Buttering up the lonely single mother so that she'd agree to move."

"No. The kiss was a mistake." He could have bitten his tongue the moment the word slipped out. "That's not what I—"

"You're right. It was a mistake. Just like coming here was a mistake," Carla spat. "I don't know what game you and your boss are playing. But count me and Nico out."

"Carla—"

"Mami. Did you see?" Nico came running to them. "I did good. Jimmy said so." Jimmy being the guy leading the pony back to the barn.

"You did wonderful, *mijito*. But we need to get ready."

While she didn't say it aloud, Philip knew she meant: get ready to leave. The tenseness of her posture and the way she refused to look at him said it all.

He regretted not telling her the truth earlier, but at least now, going forward, she would know. Lot of good that would do if she departed, though.

"I thought practice wasn't until after lunch," Nico exclaimed, climbing through the rails.

"About the tryout—"

Philip interrupted. "This visit isn't just about the soccer team, it's about the school, too. How about I give you and your mother a tour? Show you the classrooms. They have an epic science lab. Machine shops. They even teach home economics."

"What's that?" Nico asked.

"Cooking classes."

"Why do I need to learn to cook? That's Mami's job."

Carla's lips quirked. "What if I'm not around to cook for you, *mijito*? One day, you'll move out."

"No, I won't. I'm gonna live with you forever and ever." Nico took off running, and she shook her head, a smile on her lips. An expression that faded when she glanced in Philip's direction.

A hand on her arm stopped Carla before she could follow her son. "He's a good boy and an excellent player. Don't let the fact we were a little underhanded in getting you here prevent you from doing what's best for him."

"Who says the Yaguara Academy is best?"

"Why don't you give it a chance and check it out for yourself."

"I won't change my mind."

"Then what do you have to worry about?"

Her lips pressed into a thin line, hard and uncompromising. And yet, despite it, it didn't take much for Philip to recall the soft yield of them when they kissed.

"Fine." She huffed a breath. "Show us your precious school. It won't change a damned thing."

The academy itself was less than a half-hour drive from the mansion and set on over one hundred acres of land, which meant numerous fields of rolling, green grass. The headmaster gave the tour, with Nico exclaiming through much of it, his excitement uncontained. Nico then showed everyone why he deserved to be at the academy, his skills on the field resulting in the other boys high-fiving him and patting him on the back.

As Nico stood amidst the students, Philip sidled close to Carla and murmured, "He fits right in."

"He does," she admitted. "But it's still a no."

"Why?"

She didn't point but turned and looked at the

stands where Oliveira stood watching. He'd shown up not long after the warm-up.

"I don't trust him."

"He's a good man." Philip could state it truthfully.

"He's being creepy."

"He likes to watch the boys play."

"Like I said, creepy." Carla stared at the man, who caught her looking. Oliveira waved. She turned her back. "Let's go. I want to grab our things and get to the motel I found online."

"Don't be an idiot." Philip's words were harsher than he'd intended. "You've got a free place to stay."

"I don't want anything from that man."

"Now you're being petty."

Carla gave Philip a dark look. "You're awfully bossy."

"Only seems that way because you argue about everything."

"You calling me a bitch?"

"Nope. I wouldn't dare. You might kill me." He winked before walking away. Let her admire his ass for once.

On the drive back to the mansion, Nico kept the conversation alive, exclaiming about the academy. Carla said little. When they arrived at the house, Owen had a swimsuit and a towel ready for Nico, who yelled, "Last one in is a rotten egg," before running off to change.

Carla hissed at Philip. "I told you I wanted to leave."

"Then you go and tell your son." Philip waved a hand in the direction of the stairs. "Explain to him why he can't stay here and have some fun."

"You're an asshole," she spat before stomping off.

Philip didn't see her the rest of that evening. Carla watched Nico in the pool, then declined an invitation to dine with Oliveira. Instead, she opted to order in a pizza so that she and Nico could spend the evening closeted in his borrowed room watching movies.

Her excuse relayed to Owen: *"We don't want to make extra work for the staff."* Which was a polite way of saying, *"I don't want to spend time with you or your boss."*

Philip could understand her reticence. What was Oliveira's deal with them? His boss had been acting strangely, starting with the fact that he'd sent Philip to bring them back.

A knock on Oliveira's office door resulted in a barked, "Come in."

Philip entered and spotted his boss standing in front of the fireplace, staring at a painting of himself as a younger man, seated next to his wife and his son as a young child. A time when they'd both been alive.

"Evening, sir."

His boss turned from the painting. "She's avoiding me, isn't she?"

No point in lying. "Yes. She doesn't trust you."

"I don't think she trusts many people."

"You're right, she doesn't, and can you blame her? We got her here by subterfuge."

"You told her?" Oliveira's gaze narrowed.

"I didn't have a choice. She was questioning too much. She would have found out eventually."

"So, she's angry."

"Very."

"I didn't know of any other way," his boss mused aloud.

"You could have asked."

"And said what?" Oliveira turned. "Knowing her, do you really think she would have accepted an invitation from a stranger?"

"No. Especially since I still don't understand why you wanted her and Nico here."

"He's an excellent candidate."

"One of hundreds. But you wanted him in particular. What makes him so special?"

"Possibly nothing. More than likely, wishful thinking," his boss replied cryptically. "What is the plan for tomorrow? I was thinking of taking the boy—"

Philip interrupted his boss. "She's going home tomorrow."

"What?" Oliveira appeared startled. "But why?"

"Because this isn't her home."

"She can't leave yet. It's too soon."

"You can't force her to stay."

Oliveira cursed and slammed the glass he held into

the fireplace. It hit the metal grate and smashed. "Damn it all. This is more complicated than expected."

"What's going on, Luiz?" Philip didn't often use his boss's first name, part of making sure he kept a professional distance, but he could see something in Oliveira's face.

The man appeared torn. Only for a moment, before the business owner's steely mien reappeared. "Nothing. I just hate seeing talent wasted due to stubbornness."

"Maybe she'll change her mind."

Luiz gave him a look, to which Philip shrugged and grinned ruefully. "Actually, I imagine she won't." Carla's obstinate nature wouldn't let her.

"How is she getting home?"

"She's probably looking up bus schedules, but I was thinking of driving them."

"Of course you will. Just like you'll remain there as coach until the final game."

"You still want me to do that?"

"The children need someone to guide them."

There was more to it than that. "You've not yet given up on Carla and the boy." Philip scrubbed his hair. "I am not lying to them anymore."

"Never asked you to. But I do expect you to keep an eye on them."

"Why?"

"Because I said so."

"Not good enough," Philip snapped.

"Then quit if you don't like it. I have nothing more to say on the matter."

Oliveira might be done, but Philip wasn't. He'd find out why his boss was acting so out of character. He'd go back tomorrow with Carla and Nico. Try not to think about the fact that he only had days left to convince Carla he wasn't an asshole, which, for some reason, ranked high in importance.

Of course, the whole convincing part might take time, which was why he found himself outside her bedroom door, fist raised to knock. Wondering what he'd say. If he'd even get a chance to speak.

CHAPTER TWELVE

CARLA LEFT Nico alone to watch a movie and went to her room to pack. Whether Philip and his boss agreed or not, she was heading home, even if she and Nico had to take the bus.

She refused to stick around, even though what Mother dug up on Oliveira made him out to be a decent guy. Self-made billionaire, he'd started out as the son of a farmer in a mountainous Brazilian town. He'd inherited the farm and then had the good fortune to discover that parts of it had a metal ore running through it. Oliveira's riches snowballed from there.

He married the daughter of a prominent banker. A love match, by all accounts, seeing as how he never remarried after his wife's death from breast cancer.

Oliveira had one son. Dead. Victim of a high-speed crash. An athlete who'd made it big in the world of soccer and let it go to his head. Booze, drugs, and the fast life.

It appeared Oliveira had spoken the truth when he said that he had no family, which made his decision to start a foundation to help kids more plausible. It didn't mean she excused his creepy way of watching Nico. Was he a closet pedophile? Did he show benevolence to the world so that he might ingratiate himself with boys?

A little snooping meant she'd discovered that she and Nico were the first prospective academy people to stay here. The staff claimed Oliveira rarely had guests. Even Philip only occasionally spent the night. He'd been working for the man for close to seven years now.

Seven. As to his usual position? Not a coach or a teacher at the academy, but Oliveira's guy Friday. According to gossip, the boss was constantly sending Philip on errands around the country, and sometimes out of it. A glorified messenger boy by the sounds of it.

And a fine liar.

She should have known the moment they pulled up to the mansion that something was off. Well, the blinders were off now. She wouldn't stay here a moment longer than necessary.

I'm going home.

Might as well since Aunt Judy had seen and heard nothing during her stay. No strange vehicles parked on the road. No more stray shootings. The van was fixed and left unmolested in her driveway.

Which was a relief. Nico was safe, their cover still secure, and yet, Carla angrily packed. To those unfamiliar with that act, it involved stuffing her things, without folding, rhyme, or reason into her luggage. She couldn't even explain why she was so pissed. Because she sure as hell was over the fact that Moore worked for Oliveira. Good for him. She had secrets, too. Even bigger ones.

The knock had her tucking her gun nearby. She padded to the door and opened it warily.

Moore stood outside and arched a brow. "Can I come in?"

"If you're here to sell me on staying, then you can forget it. I'm going home."

"You're still peeved."

"What gave it away?" she snapped.

"Don't be mad. I came clean and told you."

She snorted. "Only 'cause you knew I would find out."

"I don't see the big deal."

"The big deal is, you dragged me to Oliveira's place and lied. Your boss hates guests."

Philip rolled his shoulders. "Hate's a strong word. He has no time for fake people."

"Yet he invites two strangers into his home. Why?"

"I don't know why. He won't tell me."

She heard the exasperation. Perhaps, finally some truth. "Is he a pedo?"

"What?"

"You heard me. Any rumors that he likes the boys? Any payoffs to families to keep their mouths shut? Come on, you're his right-hand man. Surely, you'd know. So, tell me, is he into little boys?"

Philip gaped at her, mouth opening and shutting. "Are you fucking kidding me? Oliveira is not a pedophile."

"But he likes kids."

"So do most people. That doesn't make them predators."

"Then his actions don't make sense." Carla turned away from him.

"How has he wronged you? By being nice? Offering Nico the opportunity of a lifetime?"

"What's he want in return? Because I don't believe for a moment he does this out of the kindness of his heart."

"Geezus, Carla. What the fuck made you so suspicious of people? Do you think I'm a perv, too? After all, I volunteered to coach."

"Are you?"

"Do I have to kiss you again to prove I'm not?" he snapped.

Maybe. That wasn't what she said, though. "Kissing me proves nothing."

"What kind of fucked-up childhood did you have?" he asked.

"The kind that included an abusive, alcoholic father."

Moore's hands clenched by his sides as he seethed. "Did he hurt you?"

"He hurt all of us. But not in that way." Her dad was too drunk to perform, a blessing according to her mother. However, his fists never faltered.

"Your experience with one douchebag shouldn't taint everyone."

"It wasn't one experience, though. Nico's father was, in many ways, worse." She put a hand on her cheek. "I still can't feel the skin here even though the fracture healed."

"He hit you." Philip seemed dumbfounded.

"Among other things." Carla shrugged.

"Good thing he's dead," Moore growled.

"Why? What is a gringo like you gonna do? Lecture him?" she snickered.

"I'm not a pussy."

"Nor are you a gangbanger. Matias was the lowest of the low. A killer. You wouldn't have stood a chance against him."

"You might be surprised. I'm tougher than you think."

She eyed him. "Doubtful." She turned her back on him. "You should leave. We have a long trip tomorrow."

He grabbed her and whirled her to face him. "I'm not leaving yet. We're not done."

"There's nothing left to say."

"Who said anything about talking?"

He mashed his lips to hers, and she thought about biting them. Nipped the bottom one, in fact. But in a way that sucked it into her mouth.

A good thing the door was shut because she shoved him against it and devoured his mouth. All day long, she'd been simmering.

Angry at this man.

Angry at herself.

She had so much emotion pent up inside.

Arousal, too.

Moore made her feel things. Brought her body to life, and after she went home tomorrow, she wouldn't see him again. Wouldn't get a chance to tear off his shirt, the buttons flying as she gripped the fabric and tore.

She didn't want to regret not having this chance to sate the need inside her. The throbbing between her thighs.

His fingers wrapped her hair, and he tugged her from his mouth. "What's happening?"

"You are going to fuck me." She nipped his chin, and her hand cupped his groin.

"I thought you were mad at me."

"I am. Very mad. Which makes me horny. Now, are you going to keep asking stupid questions, or are you going to do something about it?"

"I don't want you to hate me."

"Then you'd better be good," she said before sucking on his lower lip.

He growled. "You are..."

"Fucking amazing. I know. Now, shut up and kiss me." Their mouths met in a hot clash of breath and teeth. He went from being pinned against the door, to her being stripped of her shirt and bra, her back against the wall, and his mouth latched onto a nipple.

He sucked. And Carla bit her tongue lest she cry out. The door was closed, but she didn't want anyone to hear.

Wanted to pretend he didn't set her on fire. But he touched her as if he knew how weak her control was around him. His every caress, kiss, and suck was determined to drive her wild. She panted as he played with her nipples. Bucked as he pulled down her pants and put his hand on her.

When he found her mouth again with his own, his fingers played with her, finding her wet and hot. He rubbed her honey against her swollen nub, and she cried out into his mouth, her hips gyrating against his hand, needing more.

"Fuck me," she gasped.

"Don't tell me what to do," he countered, even as he helped her wrap her legs around his waist. He kept her pressed against the wall, one arm holding her body while his free hand guided his cock to the opening of her sex. He teased for a moment, rubbing the swollen head against her nether lips.

Fucking teased her.

"Give it to me," she demanded.

He thrust into her, the thickness of his cock filling her. Stretching her. She dug her fingers into his shoulder and used it as leverage to bounce herself. He helped by putting his hands on her ass, cupping her cheeks, and she threw her head back at the exquisite sensation of her cunt tugging at his prick.

She let him control their pace, especially since he'd found the angle that brought sharp jolts of ecstasy each time he hit it. His deep strokes were hard. Rhythmic. Her orgasm coiled inside. A tightly wound spring that got more intense each time he rammed in his cock.

"Yes. Yes." The only word she could manage to hiss.

As for him, he panted. His breathing ragged as he ground into her, his fingers digging into her flesh as he rammed into her harder, faster.

On the edge of bliss, she opened her eyes to find him staring at her.

Intense.

Intimate.

And still, he pumped her, his cock slamming in and out of her until her body tightened around him and she came. Came with her head thrown back, her mouth wide-open in a silent scream.

Her body racked with pleasure that left her limp in his arms.

Weak.

Vulnerable.

He took advantage, placing soft kisses on her temple.

The nerve.

Yet, for a moment, she wanted to give in. Wanted to stay within the confines of Philip's arms.

Weakness!

She shoved away from him, extricating herself from the intimate joining, feeling the cooler air of the room kissing her dewy skin.

She flipped her hair back and dug deep to find herself: tough Carla, the one who fucked and moved on. "Thanks."

"Thank you," he replied in a husky tone, moving towards her.

She danced out of reach. "Oh, no you don't. We're done."

"Done?" His tone was flat. "You're kicking me out?"

"Well, yeah. It is my room. And I was going to bed."

"You want a bed, we can do a bed," he growled.

"I'm going to be alone."

"So that's it? Wham, bam, thank you, ma'am?"

She could hear the hurt under the seething anger. "I had an itch, you scratched it. This changes nothing between us."

His lips pressed tight. "It changes everything, Carla. And you know it."

"Don't be one of those guys. I hate clingy."

"It's not clingy to want to care."

"Except I never asked you to care." Words that sounded false for some reason. For a moment, in his arms, she'd felt what it might be like to be cherished. She'd liked it.

Which was why she shoved him out the door and leaned on it.

Eyes closed.

Heart heavy.

Caring too much.

Don't make that mistake again.

CHAPTER THIRTEEN

THE FOLLOWING DAY, Carla had her bags by the door and ate her breakfast in near silence. Nico chattered enough for all of them. Oliveira had joined them, and every time he directed a word at Carla, she gave him a look.

Philip's boss tried only once to convince her to stay. With a direct stare that would have shriveled most men, she replied, "Thanks for the offer, but I think Nico and I should go home. He's got a big game coming up that he can't miss."

Then, Oliveira made the mistake of saying, "Nico performed very well yesterday. I'd like—"

"I don't think your school is a good fit."

To which, Nico blustered, "But, Mami—"

"No." Said quite firmly. She stood and placed her linen napkin on the table. "It's time to leave."

Anger and disappointment warred for predominance on Oliveira's face. He wasn't used to being ignored.

Nico tried once more. "I like it here."

She didn't speak. A pointed look at Nico brought a sigh from the kid. He stood more slowly, but rather than leave right away, he held out his hand to Oliveira. "Thank you for letting us stay. I really like your house. Your school. And your waffles." Then he hugged the older man before fleeing, leaving Oliveira gaping.

Carla, on the other hand, didn't hug or thank Oliveira. She glared. "I ever catch you lurking around my kid, I will bury you somewhere in the desert."

Philip wasn't entirely sure she was kidding.

She left, and Oliveira grumbled, "She is very stubborn. Doesn't she realize the opportunity I'm offering?"

"She does, she just doesn't care." Philip shrugged.

"I only need a few more days," his boss complained.

"I don't think a few more days would have convinced her. I should go." Before Carla made good on her promise to take a bus.

The luggage was already loaded, and Nico in the backseat, headphones on, head bopping, when Philip emerged. Carla leaned against the car and arched a brow. "Any last-minute attempt to change my mind?"

"I don't think there's much point, do you?" There was no sign of the passionate woman he'd held in his arms the night before. Had it truly meant so little to her? Would someone give him a kick in the ass for giving a damn she didn't?

"Your boss is hiding something."

On that, he didn't disagree. The strange part was Oliveira not sharing it with him. "We all hide parts of ourselves."

The response earned him a sharp look. "Is this your way of admitting you're still lying to me?"

"Everyone is allowed to have some secrets."

"Is this your way of making yourself seem mysterious?"

"I am what you see. A man doing the job he was trained for, muddling his way through life. What about you?"

Her lips twitched. "I am an undercover assassin for a secret organization that offers vigilante services to eliminate shitheads."

He laughed. "I totally approve of the vigilante part. But I have a hard time picturing you as an assassin."

"Because girls can't be killers."

"On the contrary, man or woman, I think we all have that capability." Some, more than others. "But even you have to admit it's a stretch going from soccer mom to ultra-spy."

"I don't spy. I kill. For money." She smiled and laughed, one of the first genuine ones he'd heard from her. "Can you imagine what the other parents would say?"

He snickered. "That you have a vivid fantasy life. I

don't suppose it comes with lingerie?"

"Black spandex, mostly."

"Still sexy. I've love to see you in it."

She arched a brow. "Is that your way of asking for a repeat of last night?"

"Would you say yes if it were?"

Before she could reply, Nico rolled down his window. "Are we leaving?"

"Yes." She cast Philip a coy look before getting into the car. Did the glance mean that she was interested in another go? He couldn't exactly ask with her son in the back.

Philip got into the driver seat, and once they got on the road, he pulled a sly move. He slid his hand onto her thigh.

Then he waited.

Would she fling it off or...?

Her hand came to rest on it.

Lightly.

He turned to look at her, only to find her facing the window. She didn't say or do anything else, but that hand stayed there. It made him feel...pretty damned good.

Hence why he kind of expected an invitation in when he finally pulled up outside her place. Instead, once he'd helped them unload, and she'd dumped everything inside her front hall, he was surprised when she faced him and said, "Thanks for the ride. Bye."

She went to enter, but he snared her arm.

"That's it?"

"Were you expecting something else?" She arched a brow. "I have a kid, remember? Which means I am not going to invite you in for a sleepover. I don't need Nico asking questions."

Which Philip could understand. It didn't help his frustration, though.

"I want to see you again." Naked. Skin flushed. Panting. Coming...

She closed the door and leaned on it. "Listen, Moore."

"My name is Philip."

"Last night was fun. But I'm not into the whole relationship and dating thing."

"Why not?" he pushed. "And don't give me the bullshit about all men being scum."

"The truth is, I like my life the way it is. I answer to myself. I don't have to clean up after another person. My closet is for me alone."

"First off, I'm not some kind of caveman who expects you to report your every move. I am a neat freak, and who says I want to share a closet with you?"

"You want to fuck me again."

He stepped closer. "Damned right, I do. I want to fuck you until your nails rake down my back, and your pussy clenches around my cock like a vise."

Her pupils dilated. "I can't have Nico seeing you in my bed."

"What time does he go to sleep?"

"Nine."

"See you at nine fifteen."

"Are you insane? You can't come over later just to bang me."

"Why not?" He pressed his body into hers, trapping her against the door. "You want no strings. How about I give you no strings?" He'd take what he could get and maybe, over time, she'd lose some of that prickly exterior.

"Are you trying to fuck me into saying I'll go back to the academy?"

"I want to fuck you because being balls-deep inside you is paradise."

Her breathing hitched. "We really shouldn't." She licked her lips.

"Which is why it will feel so fucking good," he whispered against her lips.

The door behind her suddenly opened, sending her stumbling.

Nico laughed. "Mami, you're never clumsy. Did Coach trip you?"

"Coach did something, all right," she grumbled.

Philip's chest swelled at the complaint. "I'll see you later," he said with a salute near his temple.

Nico grinned. "I'll be ready for practice, Coach."

Whereas, Carla, she said nothing.

But when he showed up that night at nine fifteen, bearing flowers—which she snorted at—she let him in. And practically dragged him to her room.

They didn't exchange any words.

She didn't want to talk, and he was fine with that. The moment the door to her bedroom shut, he pulled her against his body and slanted his mouth hard over hers. He'd been thinking of this moment for hours.

Wondering if it would feel as explosive as the first time.

His body ignited, and she joined him in the passion, her mouth taking a fierce turn, sucking on his bottom lip, their tongues tangled and hot. Her hands curled around his neck, and she melted into his body.

He tightened his arms around her, the feel of her lithe frame against his driving him insane. In a smooth move, he scooped her up and carried her to the bed. He followed her down, covering her body with his own. Her thighs spread, letting him nestle between them. Her hips thrust against him, a decadent friction even with the layers of clothing separating them. He ground himself against her, applying even more pressure, and she panted against his mouth.

"Fuck me," she whispered.

Philip didn't understand why every dirty word out of her mouth was such a turn on.

"You want me," he said, moving his mouth to lavish attention on the shell of her ear.

She writhed under him. "Don't make me tie you to this bed."

"Why not?" was his reply before he nipped her lobe.

Her hands found the edge of his shirt and moved underneath, stroked the flesh of his back. When she tugged at the fabric, he reared far enough back to pull off his shirt.

She raked her nails down his chest, scraping them over his nipples, which hardened into points. She pinched one, and his hips jerked.

A smile pulled her lips as she pinched the other. "Come here," she said in a husky voice, grabbing him around the neck and pulling him down.

Philip was more than happy to kiss Carla again, but at the same time, he braced himself on one arm, leaving himself with a free hand to roam. It seemed only fair that since he was shirtless, she should join him. He tugged at her shirt, inching it upward, his fingers tracing the smooth skin up her ribcage to the rounded swell of her breast.

Cupping the perfect handful, he squeezed, and she gasped against his mouth. His calloused fingers grasped her nipple, pulled it, eliciting another sound from her. He rolled the erect nub, loving how she panted faster and harder.

He leaned to the side and yanked at her shirt, pulling it over her head, baring her to his view. The previous night, he'd not gotten to enjoy her body.

It had been over too quickly.

This time, he planned to worship every inch.

He massaged her breasts, teasing first one, then the other, playing with her nipples until they stood at attention. Only then did he swoop in to capture a nub in his mouth. He sucked, and she arched, stifling her cries of pleasure with a fist in her mouth.

He sucked some more, raked the edge of his teeth along the sensitive flesh, and a low moan rolled from her. She reacted so beautifully to his touch.

His mouth slid down the taut skin of her belly. Right to the edge of her pants. It didn't take long to remove them. The panties soon followed.

Bared to his view, he couldn't help a sigh of appreciation. "You are fucking hot."

"Show me," she invited, twitching her hips. Her legs spread a little wider.

"Bossy, even in bed," he grumbled good-naturedly.

"I want to feel you inside me," she stated, sliding her hand between her legs, rubbing herself, the tips of her fingers wet.

The smell of her arousal reached him, and his cock pulsed in his pants. It wanted to sink inside her. Feel the heat of her squeezing. But first...

He caressed the smooth skin of her thighs. She trembled. He laid a kiss on the soft skin. Then another, moving from her knee upward.

"Yes," she moaned as he reached the vee of her thighs. Only, he teased her and started placing kisses on the opposite side.

She pulled her legs wide for him, knees bent, exposing herself.

He took advantage, cupping her buttocks in his palms, lifting her, tasting her. So damned sweet.

His tongue slid between her nether lips. Touched her. Stroked her. He flicked it against her clit, and she trembled.

Mewled.

He could feel how close she was by the tautness in her body. He kept lapping at her swollen button and slid a finger into her. Then a second. Feeling her flex tightly around him.

He pumped that finger, in and out. Kept licking her. Held her. Listened as her breathing grew fast and shallow.

When she came, she thrust a pillow over her face to yell, and her body convulsed. The waves of her pleasure rocked his fingers.

He quickly yanked at his pants and slid into her while she was still coming. The pillow went flying, and she reached for him. Grabbed him and yanked him down.

She kissed him deeply, passionately as he pushed himself into her.

Then pulled out.

In again, feeling the glorious heat of her orgasm still going.

He slid out and left only the tip of his cock against her lips. He slid in again slowly, and her hands clawed at his back as her hips thrust, urging him to go deeper.

He took his damned time getting there, and once

he could go no farther, he began to grind himself against her. Pushing over and over while she whimpered into his mouth.

Her body tightened. And her second orgasm was even stronger than the first.

It fisted him so tightly, it was almost painful. Then, he was coming, too. Spilling inside her, hot and without thought, the condom still in his pocket. And he didn't care.

He'd just experienced heaven.

He collapsed beside her, breathing hard. Only to gasp when she rolled on top of him.

"Not bad."

"Not bad?" he repeated. "You came twice."

"But you didn't. Got the energy to see if we can change that." He did.

He made her come again, too, so hard, she almost sobbed.

It was the best sex he'd ever had. He could have spent the night wrapped around Carla, making love to her again and again.

But that wasn't part of her plan. When he began to doze off, she poked him awake and shoved him out of bed. "Go, before we fall asleep and Nico finds you."

Philip thought it best not to mention the next time he saw her that, as he tiptoed out of her room, he ran into Nico in the hall coming from the bathroom.

Philip put a finger to his lips, and the boy grinned.

At least one person was on Philip's side.

CHAPTER FOURTEEN

THE NEXT MORNING, Carla's alarm went off and she had a moment of disorientation. She woke from a dream where she snuggled with Philip. And it wasn't horrible.

Which made the reality all the lonelier as she woke to a bed completely mussed but empty of the man who had taken her to such blissful heights.

I can't believe he came to see me. Carla hadn't truly thought he would return— with fucking flowers as if it were a date.

She'd almost sent him packing. How dare he ignore the fact that she didn't want a relationship. How dare he treat her like a girlfriend.

The horror.

But, at the same time, she'd experienced an inner giddy pleasure especially since she'd been thinking about him for hours, remembering how it had felt to have him inside her. Wondering if the second time could be as good as the first.

When he walked in the door, she'd barely been able to contain herself. Dragging him to her bedroom like a nympho starving for sex.

Not that he'd minded. His passion equaled hers.

And it was even better than the first time. So good, Carla relaxed and had begun to doze off, which would have been a disaster. What if she'd not managed to kick him out before morning? Nico would have then seen Philip. How to explain that Mommy was just using Nico's coach for sex?

She really should say no to a next time. Because there *would* be a next time if Philip had meant the kiss he'd dropped on her lips, and the whispered, "See you tomorrow," as he left.

Now that was all she could think about as she showered and got ready for work. As her hands soaped her tender body, it vibrated, already aching for another round.

Absolute madness. Since when did she ever want seconds? Probably some almost-thirty sexual crisis. She could handle it. It wouldn't be the first time her removable showerhead helped her out.

However, the tiny orgasm did little to sate, and she ran late getting ready for work. Thankfully, Nico didn't need much help dressing for school. She insisted on dropping him off rather than letting him take his bike, using the excuse of picking him up after school for the newly scheduled practice.

"Don't talk to strangers," she admonished as she let him out in front of the school, ignoring the angry stares from the parents she blocked.

"I'm not a baby, Mom," he stated, forgoing his usual *Mami* with his tween irritation.

Thing was, he would always be her baby. The good news was that she saw nothing suspicious at all during her trip to the school and to work.

Perhaps life could go back to normal. A new normal that involved a hot, temporary coach.

She had to remind herself that once the big game was over, he'd return to his home and regular job. Heck, she wondered if Philip would even stick around now for the final game this weekend given that Oliveira didn't get what he wanted.

She sure hoped Philip didn't leave the kids in the lurch. They'd worked so hard.

Going in to work felt surreal—and boring. Carla spent the day pushing paper around, not getting much done. Counting the minutes, and hours, until she could leave.

Unlike some at her company who worked out of cubicles, her results when it came to denying claims meant an office—albeit a tiny one with barely enough room to move around—with a door, which people usually knocked on.

Suddenly, it swung open and hit the wall with a bang as someone loomed in the entrance, setting off her danger meter. Her hand reached under her desk and curled around the grip of the gun she kept hidden there.

A big man hulked in the doorway. In his thirties, maybe older, hard to tell amidst the tattoos and the sneer on his tanned face. His bald pate even bore some ink, and golden hoops dangled from each ear.

He eyed her. "Well, lookie here. The *puta* is back in town."

"Who are you?" she snapped, not recognizing the man. "Get out of my office before I call security." Her inner thoughts went more along the lines of, *Get your ass out of here or I will blow a hole in your head.* She could claim self-defense. It wouldn't be hard to stage. She could quite easily claim that he threatened her given she kept a second unmarked gun in her purse that she could quickly slip into his limp, dead hand.

However, staying under the radar meant not blowing holes in people who couldn't mind their manners. Fucking laws.

Rather than obey her demand to leave, the thug slammed the door shut and dropped into the lone chair in front of her desk. "I ain't going anywhere, *puta*. You and I have business to discuss."

"If this is about an insurance claim, then you need to make an appointment. We don't accept drop-in visits."

"This is about family, Carlotta Lopez."

Her blood froze at the use of her old name. The one she had been born with and had left behind eleven years ago. She didn't let her unease show. She did, however, tug the gun onto her lap. "I am afraid you have the wrong person."

"No, I don't. I seen enough pictures of you when I was in the clink to know you by sight. My brother liked to visit me in the pen and brag about his hot *puta*."

Brother. The horrifying realization hit Carla. "You're Pedro." Matias's older brother. A man she'd never met. Pedro was in jail before she and Matias had started dating.

He leaned back in his seat with a smug smile. "I see you're starting to get your memories back."

"What do you want? How did you find me?" Because Carlotta no longer existed. Not a single database. School record. Nothing. Mother had ensured it was all wiped clean.

"Fate must love me because I saw you pulling out of a parking lot a few weeks ago and I thought, fuck me, that looks just like Matias's whore of a girlfriend."

Coming face-to-face with someone from her past brought a sour taste to Carla's mouth. "I'm not his girlfriend," she spat. She was stronger than that girl. Smarter, too.

"'Course you're not, 'cause he's dead."

She bit her tongue before she uttered *"good riddance."*

The chair creaked as he leaned forward. "Thing is, word on the street is you did it."

"You shouldn't listen to rumors."

"I know it's bullshit because I can't see Matias getting taken out by a little *puta* like you. But I do think you probably spread your legs for another guy and used your pussy to convince him to do the job for you."

Just like a man to think a woman couldn't act for herself.

"What do you want? To insult me? Because I really don't give a fuck what you think."

"Seems kind of unfair that you're alive while my brother is dead and alone in heaven."

"You can't seriously think your asshole of a brother is in heaven." Carla couldn't help the derisive laughter even as her words goaded Pedro to anger.

He slapped her desk. "Don't fuck with me, *puta*. I will wring your neck and not give a shit."

"Your parole officer might have a problem with that." A wild guess on her part, but Pedro looked like the type who spent his whole life on probation. "Does the officer know you like harassing women? Maybe I should give him a call."

Pedro leaned back in his seat, a cold smile on his lips. "I wouldn't do that if I were you. Anything happens to me, and you're screwed. My friends know all about you. You and my nephew. Nico, isn't it?"

Fear and anger warred for dominance. "You leave my son alone."

"Your son? Have you forgotten he's my family, too? That's my nephew, and I think it's about time he met his father's side. And there ain't fuck all you can do about it."

"I'm his mother, and you're just a shithead of an uncle. You have no rights."

"I will if the kid ends up an orphan." Said with a menacing leer.

Enough was enough. Carla pulled the gun from her lap and aimed it at Pedro's face. "You listen to me, asshole, and listen good. You will stay away from me and Nico. Because if you don't, I'll kill you and they'll never find your body."

He spread his arms wide. "You don't have the *cojones* to kill me."

"Don't be so sure of that. You know those rumors about me killing your brother? I didn't hire anyone. It was me." She leaned forward and whispered, "And I liked it."

Finally, a frown marred Pedro's brow. "You're bluffing, *bitch*." His heavy accent hit the *b* hard.

"Am I?" Carla pulled back the hammer of the gun and smiled. "I shoot you, and everyone will believe my story of the big, bad thug who threatened me. The mean man who's been stalking me. Because it was you, wasn't it? Taking potshots at my van. Slashing my tires."

His visage twisted. "Yeah, it was me, and I will do worse before I'm done."

"No, you won't. Because the next time you show your face, I'll put a bullet in it."

"You are making a mistake," he growled, heaving out of the chair.

Carla kept the gun trained on him. "No, you're the one making the mistake. You leave me and my son alone, or you will join your brother in hell."

"This isn't over," Pedro threatened as he left her office.

Left her shaking like she'd not shaken in years.

She wasn't imagining shit. Pedro had threatened her and Nico.

We have to leave. The panic hit Carla like she'd not felt since her time with Matias.

Exiting her office, she barked to those who asked her where she was going, "Home. I'm sick."

She sped to Nico's school and spent an impatient moment in the office as they had him fetched from his class. She paced out front, eyes on the street until he joined her.

Would Pedro hit now or later?

When her son emerged, he frowned. "What's wrong, Mami?"

"We have to go."

"Go home, now?" he queried. "Why?"

"Not home. We need to leave the city. Today."

Only as she reached the van did she realize he wasn't following. He stood a few yards away, an angry look on his face. "I can't leave. I have practice."

"Sorry, *mijito*, but this is important."

"Why? What happened?"

"I can't say. Get in the van."

He got in, his face sullen, but he wasn't done. "I don't want to leave."

"There's danger if we stay."

"Danger how?"

How to explain that his psycho father's even more psycho brother was gunning for them? Or her, at least, but she wouldn't put it past Pedro to hurt Nico to get at her.

"Someone at Mommy's work is angry."

"So call the police."

"The police can't help us."

"I don't want to leave. I can't. My team needs me."

The anguish in his words tore at her. How could she let her past mistakes hurt him? And what the hell was she thinking running?

Pedro was just a thug.

Not even a smart or sophisticated one. So why the fuck was Carla letting Pedro win? She had taken down bigger assholes than him. She was the one who should be instilling fear and exacting retribution. Did it really only take the blustering threats of one bully to destroy a decade of training?

She patted her son's knee. "You're right, *mijito*. We shouldn't let a bad guy chase us away. This is our home."

Which was why the moment they got home, she sent out a group chat.

Soccer Mom: *Hey, gals, long time no see. I was wondering if you want to come for a visit and watch Nico's big game this weekend.*

Hockey Mom: *Sure. It's off-season for me, and Junior is due for a visit with Grandma.*

Frenemy Mom: *Can't. Little tadpole in the oven is making travel queasy. But I might send Declan. He's driving me nuts.*

Soccer Mom: *LOL. Better keep him at home because you know he'll just be texting nonstop to check on you.*

Tiger Mom: *I can't get a sitter, and it's been a while since our kids visited. Do you have room for the twins?*

Soccer Mom: *Sure. Aunt Judy has some extra beds.*

Cougar Mom: *Just finishing my trip in the Bahamas and would love an excuse not to go home quite yet. Empty nesting sucks!*

Soccer Mom: *Can't wait to see you.*

Slipping her phone into her pocket, a sense of relief—and evil satisfaction—filled Carla. Pedro didn't know who he'd fucked with. She'd just called in the cavalry, and if there was one thing you never fucked with, it was a Killer Mom's kid.

CHAPTER FIFTEEN

AS PHILIP RAN the boys through their practice, he couldn't help being distracted.

Carla had arrived last, and even from his spot on the field, he could see the tension in her. The way she scanned everything and everyone. What had her on edge? More vandalism?

He had to wonder, because that afternoon, he'd had to deal with his irritated boss.

"Have you talked to her about coming back yet?" Oliveira barked without saying hello.

"We haven't even been back a day. Give her some time."

"I've already wasted too much time," his boss muttered.

"You're not making sense."

"You'll understand soon. I'll explain everything once you're back."

"Why not tell me now?"

"I have my reasons."

Reasons Philip couldn't fathom, which was why he had no intention of pressuring Carla into returning to Pasadena. At least not for Oliveira. If Philip asked her to move, it would be for another reason entirely.

Despite having known her for only a few days, he was falling for the woman, prickly nature and all. Liked her enough that he'd yet to decide if he would go back home once the coaching gig was done. Staying, though, meant quitting his job, but he'd socked away enough money that he could float for quite some time. He could always pick up an odd job here and there.

But all that was premature-thinking, given Carla's view on dating and men.

For all Philip knew, last night truly was the last time they'd be together. He hoped not.

When the practice ended, he sauntered over to Carla, hands in pockets, attempting to look casual, hiding his irritation at every parent that tried to get in his way. Yapping about the big game. Asking all kinds of questions.

He might have been more abrupt than necessary, which meant they'd complain. Let them. There was only one big game left for him to coach, then they could harass whoever was hired for the following season.

As Philip neared Carla, she didn't acknowledge

him, her gaze still intent on the road as Nico tossed his stuff into the van.

"Hey," he said.

"Hey." Spoken without turning to look at him.

It rubbed him wrong, even as he recognized her tense posture. "What's wrong?"

"Nothing is wrong." She bald-faced lied. Anyone could see that something had her on edge.

"I'm not an idiot. Something has you freaked out." Because her actions were those of a person on high-alert.

"Nothing I can't handle."

As reassuring statements went, it fell flat. Carla thought she could deal, alone, with whatever had her jumpy as a cat. For some reason, it roused Philip's anger. "Are you being threatened?"

"I said I can handle it." She pushed away from her van, her hands tucked into her pockets, her bulky sweater slouching over them.

"Would it kill you to let me help you?"

"Possibly." She grinned. And then, to his surprise, she went on tiptoe and gave him a quick kiss on the cheek. "Thanks for giving a shit. But I am seriously fine."

"I'm not. You're driving me crazy."

"I thought that was a good thing." The woman threw him off-kilter with a wink.

"Does that mean I can see you later?" he asked as she walked around the van.

"Why not?" She gave him a look. "Same time?"

He was there by nine fourteen, sharp. This time with a six-pack of beer.

She shoved them into the fridge and then she was all over him.

They barely made it to her room, their passion proved so fierce. Round two, he made sure to enjoy a more leisurely exploration in bed.

Once again, she kicked him out at an ungodly hour.

But he didn't complain. The fact of the matter was, Carla hadn't said no to him. Which was why he felt pretty confident in saying, "See you tomorrow," as he prepared to leave.

"Can't do tomorrow. My girlfriends are visiting from out of town, so I'm gonna have a full house."

"Embarrassed of me?" he prodded.

"More like I wasn't going to submit you to their curiosity. But if you think you can handle it..." she teased.

"Same time as usual?"

"Sure. And if you feel a need to bring something, bring ice cream. Salted caramel or cherry cheesecake, or both."

"Not wine?"

"We don't drink."

He'd lose his man card for admitting it; however, he felt a certain excitement at her invitation. Willing to introduce him to her friends. A big step. Not that he made a big deal of it.

He played it cool as he left, giving her a hot kiss that left her with heavy-lidded eyes and a smile.

He returned the next day, same time as usual, with a few cartons of ice cream in a bag, and a box of chocolates tucked between his arm and body.

There were two cars parked out front and in the driveway. One with out-of-town plates, the other a rental.

He fought an urge to check his appearance and lightly knocked.

The door was answered by a blonde, her hair pulled back in a ponytail, her expression bright and curious. "Hi."

"Hi. Um, I'm Philip. A friend of Carla's," he stated.

"I know who you are. We've been waiting for you."

The way she said it made him wonder what he'd walked into. Especially since there was music playing, an instrumental jazz piece.

"I brought goodies," he said, lifting the bag.

"So did we." A big smile pulled her lips as she sang, "Carla, your boyfriend is here."

"He's not my boyfriend," Carla exclaimed, appearing behind the blonde and giving her a playful shove. "He's my fuck buddy."

He didn't know if he should die of embarrassment on the spot or be glad that at least she didn't pretend they were nothing. Fuck buddy was better than nobody.

"He's cute," remarked a very well put-together

older woman who eyed him up and down. "Preppier than I would have expected you to go for. More my type, as a matter of fact."

"Down, Meredith. He's mine."

Again, said in a lighter, teasing tone than he'd ever heard from Carla before. He especially liked the *mine* part.

Philip entered and said in an aside to Carla, "Where's Nico?"

"He is staying at my aunt Judy's. My friend Portia came into town with her girls, so he's visiting with them. You'll meet her later."

"Oh."

"And now to introduce you to the ladies. That cougar trying to size you up is Meredith. Watch her hands, she likes to grab ass, and it would be a shame if I had to cut them off," Carla joked.

Meredith snorted. "Your knife skills aren't that good, so I'd like to see you try."

"The one who can't pronounce *about* and drops *eh's* like they're going out of style is Tanya."

"I'm surprised you didn't tell him I live on poutine and beavertails," the Canadian woman said with a roll of her eyes.

"I was saving that for later. Girls, this is Philip. Nico's coach, and my fuck buddy."

What could a man say to that kind of intro? "Hi. Nice to meet you."

Meredith eyed him and pursed her lips. "So, he's

the one who conned you into checking out that academy?"

"The one and only."

"Must be some good dick," Meredith noted.

The frankness made him wonder if he should run away. But he was made of sterner stuff.

The ice cream and chocolate were taken from him, and he was shoved into taking a seat on the couch. Carla took a spot beside him, while the other two perched across from them and bombarded him with questions.

"Where did you grow up?"

"Tell us about your family."

"What did you study in college?"

Mostly basic stuff that he easily answered while his gaze often sought out Carla, who was more relaxed than he'd ever seen her. She leaned against the armrest of the couch, half turned, with her feet tucked against his legs.

He began tossing his own questions back. "How did you guys become friends?"

That caused them to share a glance with each other before Carla shrugged. "We attended the same camp."

"In Canada," Tanya snickered.

"Were you the camp instructor?" he asked the older woman.

"Not exactly. I was a returning attendee when they were there," Meredith explained.

"What kind of camp?"

"Survival training. For girls only." Carla stood and went into the kitchen before returning with a few glasses filled with a golden liquid. She handed one to Philip.

"It's fresh lemonade," Tanya said. "Portia made it earlier."

"Because she's a total tiger mom who is always watching everything we eat. Natural this and natural that," Carla mocked.

"Processed foods are bad for us." Tanya rose to the missing friend's defense.

"But they taste so good," Carla remarked.

"Until you get older, then they're the devil's food," Meredith chimed in.

As for Philip, he stayed out of the debate and took a large gulp. It could have used more sugar given its tartness.

"It's good." Would have been better with vodka, though.

"Have you ever played Never Have I Ever?" Tanya asked.

"I know of it. Why?"

"Because we're going to play." Tanya clapped her hands.

Meredith dangled her glass. "I'll start. Never have I ever eaten a beavertail."

As Tanya took a big sip of her drink, he couldn't help a grimace. "Is that a Canadian delicacy?" he asked.

Carla chuckled. "She's fucking with you. It's a pastry they make fried in oil and dipped in icing."

Tanya giggled. "It messes with the tourists."

"My turn." Tanya held up her glass. "Never have I ever skinny-dipped."

The women groaned as Meredith tilted back her beverage. He joined her.

When Carla gaped, Philip shrugged. "What? Haven't you?"

"No. I live in the city. Where am I going to swim naked?"

The questions went on and on. With him drinking for many of them, but he wasn't alone. He ended up with a second glass when the statements took an odd turn.

"Never have I ever killed someone," Carla stated. Then drank. As did Tanya and Meredith.

He hesitated before drinking, too. Then laughed. "I take it we're counting bugs and rodents."

"Some of them were definitely roaches," snickered Tanya.

"I think we're ready," was Meredith's cryptic reply.

"How long have you been working for Oliveira?" Carla asked.

The query made him frown since he was fairly sure he'd already told her, and it didn't seem part of the game. "Seven years."

"And your real name is Philip Moore?" Meredith put down her glass.

"Philip John Moore, the second. My dad has delusions of grandeur," he admitted before taking another sip.

"How old are you?" Tanya's turn.

"Thirty-seven. And before you ask, I'm a Taurus." He relaxed as he let them conduct their interview. Apparently, it was the get-to-know-the-fuck-buddy portion of the evening. Let them question. He still saw it as a good sign that Carla had let him meet her friends.

"What branch of the military did you work for?"

How did they know? "Special Ops, Delta Force." He spilled the secret and blinked.

Carla exchanged a glance with Meredith, who stood and drew closer. "How long did you serve?"

None of your business. The words he should have said. Instead, "I joined at nineteen and did eight years before I retired."

"Why did you leave?"

"Because my commanding officer was an asshole who didn't give a shit about his men. And I got annoyed that the truly bad men weren't the ones we were ordered to take out." The truth blurted from him, and anger filled him as he spilled closely guarded secrets. What the fuck was wrong with him?

He stared at his glass, then at Carla, who still watched him.

"What did you do to me?"

"Truth serum."

"Fuck off." He didn't believe her, even as his tongue loosened some more, making him almost blurt out how pretty she looked right now.

Her expression said she was serious. "Tanya slipped it into your drink."

Anger flared hotly inside him. "What the fuck, Carla? Why?"

"Because I don't like secrets."

He growled. "Some secrets are not supposed to be revealed. I signed documents to keep quiet about my time in the military."

"A career you never told me about."

"Because you didn't ask," he snapped.

"Would you have told me?"

"No." The word blurted from him. "It's not something I like to talk about."

"And yet it makes you that much more interesting," Carla noted, moving to kneel before him. "You were a sniper."

"Yes." He hissed.

"How many did you kill?"

"Too many."

"Did they deserve it?"

He closed his eyes and clenched his jaw, but the truth kept spilling. "Some did."

"Do you have nightmares? Regrets?"

"There are always regrets." But bad dreams or the PTSD that so many others suffered? Maybe he lacked something, some kind of empathy, because one of the reasons he excelled at his job was because he didn't feel a thing. He did as he was told and slept like a baby afterwards. However, he did eventually become choosy about whom he'd kill. When the day came that his commanding officer ordered him to kill someone, a woman whose only crime was being married to the wrong guy, he'd said no and walked away.

"What do you know of me and Nico?"

"You're hot. He's a cool kid."

One of her friends giggled.

"What's my name?"

"Carla Baker."

"My other name?"

He frowned. "What other name?"

"Do you know Pedro?"

"No. Who is he?"

"A bad shit. Are you here to take my son from me?"

"No." He would never. "But Oliveira wants him. Both of you."

"Why?"

"I don't know." What he did know was that he needed to get out of there. Needed to escape before Carla asked the right question and he spilled things that should never be revealed.

He stood, and his head spun.

"Where are you going?" Carla asked.

"Away."

"Away where?"

"Anywhere away from you. This isn't cool."

"I've got a question for him," said Meredith. "Do you like Carla?"

"Yes."

"Do you love her?"

"Tanya!" Carla screeched.

He bit his lip rather than reply because the startling truth was, he might. And this even though he couldn't walk in a straight line.

An arm went around his waist. Steadied him. "Let's get you to bed."

"No." He went to shove away from Carla, but she proved stronger than expected. She kept him anchored and guided him up the stairs to her room, then dumped him on her mattress.

He glared at her, lacking the coordination to rise. "Why?" A word that barely made it past his sluggish lips.

"I had to be sure you weren't working against me, especially once I found out that you were ex-military."

"You could have asked," he said, struggling to keep his eyes open.

"I couldn't take the chance you'd lie."

"Wouldn't lie to you," was the final truth he whispered before he couldn't fight the darkness any longer.

CHAPTER SIXTEEN

AS PHILIP'S EYES SHUT, Carla brushed the hair from his temple, allowing herself a moment to stare at him.

How could she not have seen the military in him? The way he held himself. The fact that he had remained calm during the drive-by shooting. Only those with training knew how to react.

The odd thing was, he didn't carry a gun. Carla had groped him enough times to know. While he did work for Oliveira, everything she'd seen thus far pointed to the man being an aboveboard businessman. Tanya had done some digging, too. No links to crime or drugs. No rumors of shady dealings. Not a single shell company to be found.

So what use did a businessman have for an ex-Special Ops sniper? She was kind of impressed by

Philip's records given they were sealed and took quite a bit of delicate hacking to get a peek at. Not that they saw much. The parts they'd managed to get ahold of showed large redacted passages. Enough to imply that Philip was more like Carla than she would have ever imagined.

But was his past enough for him to accept her as she was? Could Philip handle her killer nature?

She should have asked while she had the chance.

A part of her felt bad about the trick she'd played on him. She didn't have much choice. Once they'd discovered his past, Carla had to know what his plans were. Had he slept with her because he wanted to, or as part of some ulterior plan?

Because Oliveira had been snooping on Carla. Safeguards were pinged as someone poked into her fabricated history. Mother had the pinger traced back to a private eye, whose bank accounts showed payments received from Oliveira's personal account.

What was the old man's interest in Carla? Was he looking for leverage to force Nico into his academy? Just how far would the bastard go? And how much involvement did Philip have?

According to the truth serum, none. Philip Moore was who he seemed. A guy who rocked her world in the bedroom and consumed her thoughts outside it.

"Everything okay?" Meredith peeked into the room.

"Yeah, just making sure he's actually sleeping."

"And feeling guilty that you drugged him."

"Yeah." Carla sighed. "Why does everything have to be so complicated?"

"Who says it has to be?"

"Because I am who I am."

"And?"

"How am I supposed to have a relationship with someone if I can't be truthful with them?"

"Did it ever occur to you that he might not care?"

She snorted. "What kind of man is going to want to hook up with a killer?"

"Another killer."

"A retired one."

"So why not retire, too?"

Give up the one thing that had defined her life for the last decade? For a man? "I don't know if I want to." Carla liked making the world a better place. Liked the money, too.

"He likes you," Meredith noted.

"Only because he has no idea who I truly am."

"Yet. But given what we've learned of him, he might be the one person in the world who can accept you as you are."

"I don't need a man."

"You don't," Meredith agreed.

"Then why...?" She couldn't articulate what she wanted. How she wanted. Wanted the happiness he made her feel. The excitement she felt when she saw his face. The comfort she enjoyed in his arms.

"Why are you falling in love?"

Gasping, Carla whirled and glared at Meredith. "I am not in love."

"Maybe not yet, but it's happening."

Her lips pressed into a thin line. "No. I won't let it."

"Why not?"

"Because." Because love hurt. Love made a person weak. And it wasn't just Carla's experience with Matias that made her think so. Her mother and father were another classic example. All the agents employed by KM had horror stories.

Yet, despite her past, Audrey had fallen in love. Which meant that Carla could, too.

"Are you seriously going to shove the chance of love aside because of a few douchebags?"

"I have Nico to think of."

"Don't use your kid as an excuse. Do you really think Nico wants you to be alone?"

Had Meredith told her that Nico needed a dad, she might have argued, but... "What if he hurts me?"

"Then kill him." Meredith shrugged. "I did that to my second husband. Two-timing bastard."

Carla blinked at Meredith.

"Oh, don't look at me like that. He wasn't a real husband. I was undercover. Deep undercover, and I liked him well enough. Until I found out he was screwing everything he could intimidate. So, I killed him. Got a nice bonus for it, too, given the agency let me keep most of the assets I inherited as his wife."

"That's cold, Merry."

"That's life. Love happens, and when it does, enjoy it to the fullest. When that love is broken, then move on."

"You make it sound easy."

"Take it from someone older than you. It can be."

"I don't know if I'm ready for love."

"But you like him."

"Yeah."

"Then enjoy it while you can. It doesn't have to be complicated unless you choose to make it complicated."

"He's gonna be pissed when he wakes up."

"Then give him a blowjob. He'll forgive you if you swallow."

"Merry!" Carla screeched.

Meredith laughed. "Don't be a prude like Tanya. The man is falling for you. And once you explain you did it to protect yourself and Nico, I doubt he'll stay mad."

"What if he figures out who I am?"

"Then either he accepts you, or—" Meredith never finished her sentence.

The sound of glass breaking drew their attention.

Carla was on Meredith's heels as they bolted down the stairs to find Tanya in the living room, gun out and aimed at the broken bay window. A brick sat in the middle of the floor.

Only a brick. The version of a gauntlet.

Pedro had just declared war.

Carla looked at her sisters and smiled. "Who's in the mood to go hunting?"

CHAPTER SEVENTEEN

WAKING up proved harder than usual. Philip fought against the grogginess trying to keep him under. Weighed down by a ton of bricks, his head and body refused to cooperate.

What happened? Did he get wasted or something? Last he recalled, he'd gone to Carla's, met her friends, and then—

The memory of what she'd done hit him. Philip sat bolt upright in bed and yelled, "Fucking bitch!"

"Is that any way to say good morning?"

His head swiveled to take in Carla, snuggled in bed beside him, a fact he just now noticed. "You fucking drugged me." Drugged him well enough that his body wanted to play dead. Even his cock didn't stir at the sight of her bare shoulder peeping from the blanket.

But then again, why would it get hard. Philip was pissed at her, and Carla showed no remorse at all.

"I did."

"To interrogate me."

"Yup." She didn't even deny it.

He struggled with his rage and incomprehension. "Why?"

"Like I said last night, I had to know if I could trust you."

"By fucking with my mind?" He rolled out of bed and staggered as the lingering effects of the serum made his vision waver. "What did you use?" Because whatever it was proved effective. He'd spilled his guts until the drug knocked him out.

"TTT43."

"Never heard of it."

"Not surprising given it hasn't hit the market quite yet. It's a new tincture derived from scopolamine. Only requires a small dosage. Works great except for the fact it knocks the subjects out."

"Not for sale, and somehow you got your hands on some."

"Yup. You might say I have friends in interesting places." She rolled onto her back in bed and stretched, the sheet falling from her trim and tanned body.

Her naked body.

Philip noticed that he was also quite nude and completely forgot what he meant to say. What was there to say as the woman in front of him transitioned into someone new. Visually, Carla hadn't changed. She still appeared the gorgeous Latina with a curve to her lips, a nicely shaped body, and a naughty twinkle in her eyes.

How dare she look so fucking happy. Why the hell did he feel answering warmth? He was pissed at her. Totally angry. Especially since he could sense that he didn't have all the pieces to the puzzle.

But the woman in front of him did. "What the fuck is going on, Carla?"

"Nothing yet. But that could change quickly if you come back to bed." She patted the mattress and offered him a seductive grin.

Damn her if it didn't get a rise. His cock said hello, and Philip growled.

"I am not in the mood."

"Your soldier begs to differ."

"It's an urge to pee."

"Pretty big urge." She winked and wiggled.

He almost joined her in bed. He glanced away instead. "Don't you play coy. What you did wasn't cool."

"The good news is you passed the interview."

"I am not interested in passing any tests," Philip snapped.

"Would you feel better if I said come back to bed so I can make it up to you?"

Yes, but he wasn't about to give in. "I am not interested in being with a woman who thinks it's okay to drug her lover."

"Lover? Is that how you see me?" She rolled to her

stomach, holding herself aloft on her elbows, meaning her breasts dipped, and the shadowed vale between them acted as a magnet. "Have to say, lovers sounds a little too nice for the dirty things we've been doing." She crawled closer to him. Close enough she had to tilt her head back to continue looking at him.

The visual proved super distracting given her lips were now so close to his cock. A cock that strained to reach her mouth.

Philip glared at Carla, wanting to stay angry. It wasn't just lust that made him want to forgive. He was kind of digging the more relaxed and playful version of her. Her sexy factor skyrocketed a few levels. What had changed?

"If you didn't trust me, then why sleep with me?" Because that was at the core of what bothered him. She obviously didn't trust—him—and with good reason.

"I had sex with you because you're hot."

His chest swelled.

"And I was horny. Still am horny, which is why I wish you'd stop talking so much and come over here."

"Stop acting as if this is no big deal." He kept his gaze averted. Tried to hold on to his anger.

She sighed. "Geez, slip a guy one little mickey, and he's all 'what the fuck' instead of doing me."

"How did you know to ask about my Special Ops career?" The realization that he'd spilled secrets he'd sworn to keep bothered him, especially since he thought himself clear of his military past.

"I have connections."

"Your girlfriends?"

"Tanya is an excellent hacker, and while she refuses to work for the government, she is damned good at getting past their firewalls."

Having a friend who was computer smart wasn't weird. "Is she the one who got you the drug, too?"

"No, that was Portia. She works for a lab."

"So, what's Meredith's specialty?"

"Distraction and backup on missions."

"What's your job, then?"

Her lips curved into a playful grin. "I'm the muscle." She flexed an arm.

He didn't give in to the flirting. "You make yourself and your girlfriends sound like a Special Ops team."

"One hundred percent covert. We call ourselves the Killer Moms."

He snorted. "Now that's original. If this is you sober, I'd hate to see you drunk."

"I am a crack shot even when plastered."

"You have a gun?"

"A gun is putting it mildly. At last count, I had over a hundred. But I don't keep them all in one place."

"Show me one. If you're such a gun nut, then you must have one lying around." He challenged her claim.

"One?" She snorted. "Try five."

As he gaped, she reached under the pillow between the mattress and the wall. Pulled out a magnum. "One." She placed it beside her before reaching into her nightstand. "Two." Another gun joined the first. She dangled over the edge of the bed, shoved a hand between the mattress and box spring. "Three."

Four was inside the lampshade when she lifted it. For the last one, she rolled to the side of the bed and dropped down, reaching under the skirt. She rose with a shotgun clasped in one hand. She laid it on the bed.

"That's just what I can reach. Want more?"

No. Because he might fall in love.

Seriously.

He'd never met a woman so comfortable with a weapon. Who kept them stashed all over the place.

Which made him frown. "Aren't you worried about Nico finding them?"

"Nico knows to leave my guns alone. He also doesn't come into my room. The other hiding spots in the house aren't as easy to find."

"Why do you need so many guns?"

"Protection."

"One is protection. A hundred is a hobby."

"I like them." She stroked the barrel of the magnum. Gripped its length, and he felt a spurt of jealousy at how she handled it.

"You can shoot them?"

"Every single one. Take them apart too, and reassemble in the dark. Does it bother you?"

"Didn't your hacker tell you? I'm a gun collector, too."

She smiled. "What's your favorite one?"

"I have a soft spot for my Walther P88."

"An antique. Nice. I actually enjoy the sound and action of loading a shotgun. Ain't worth shit in a real fight, but for intimidation..." She sighed wistfully.

"What do you need protection from?" Because he didn't believe for a minute her story of being some kind of enforcer. More likely, she teased him. It was working.

"My enemies. Past clients from jobs. People really just don't get that, sometimes, business is just business. Then there're mistakes from your past that resurface and think they can be an asshole." Her expression darkened.

"Who showed up? Are you being threatened?" Instantly, his rage at her evaporated.

"Yes. Matias's brother, Nico's uncle, Pedro, decided to make an appearance in my office a few days ago."

It shocked Philip that she finally told him. "Why the fuck didn't you say so?"

Her shoulders rolled. "Because I wasn't sure I could trust you. You work for Oliveira."

"And?"

"I wanted to be sure you weren't using me to advance his agenda."

"I don't know what he's up to." Which didn't sit well, but he did possess one certainty. "Oliveira might be a lot of things, but he's not a bad shit. If he was, I wouldn't work for him."

She shrugged. "Says you. I had to be sure. I don't take chances when it comes to Nico."

"And it took a drug to convince you?"

"It worked. I know you're not using me."

It was underhanded. Over the top. Yet, looking at Carla now, relaxed, even joking, could he say it wasn't worth it? "What does this uncle want?"

"Revenge for his brother's death. He also wants Nico because they're blood. But I will kill him before that happens."

"I'm going to take a wild guess and say Pedro is a thug."

"Pedro is a killer like his brother. He only toyed with me because he thought I'd be an easy target to scare. He's about to learn that's not the case."

"You need protection." Philip could do that. Make that he *would* protect because no one was allowed to hurt her.

"No, what I need is you in that shower."

She rolled from the bed and walked naked to the bathroom. He couldn't help but follow. The shower appeared small. It got even smaller when he climbed in with her.

"I'm still pissed at you," he stated, placing his hands on her waist.

She tilted her head back, letting the water sluice

her hair. She braced her palms on his chest and leaned close. "Would it help if I said I'm sorry?"

Actually, it would. As did the kiss she placed on his lips.

The reaction was instant. His arms locked around her and embraced her back. He couldn't remain angry at this woman. Couldn't help finding himself more intrigued than ever.

Wouldn't it just be the wildest thing ever if she truly were a killer? Not likely, but if she were, then he might have found the one woman who wouldn't shy away from the dark parts of his life.

He lifted her and moved her, not easy in the tight stall, and pushed her back against the wall. The warm spray of the shower hit his ass. Her legs parted, and he thrust a hand between them, rubbing a finger along the moist shell of her sex.

She moaned into his mouth. Then nipped him. "Give me a sec while I do something." She crouched, and he almost lost his balance in her shower-tub combo. He grabbed hold of the shower curtain rod and groaned as she took the head of him into her mouth.

"Yes." He hissed the word as she began to bob, sliding her lips back and forth along the length of him. Her cheeks hollowed with suction. Her perfect mouth opened wide to accommodate his size.

He reached and stroked her slick hair. Cupping the back of her head. Encouraging her but not forcing. He didn't need to. She blew him with eagerness.

And just before he came?

She rose and turned around, giving him her ass. She pushed it against his groin, nudging his rigid cock. "Fuck me, soldier."

"Yes, ma'am." He grabbed her around the waist, and she parted her thighs, tilting her butt even more, presenting herself to him.

The head of his shaft probed the pink mouth of her sex. He rubbed it, spreading her lips as she braced her hands on the wall.

He slid in. Nice and slow. He felt the slickness of her channel. The trembling.

He sheathed himself fully and stopped.

She wiggled.

He sucked in a breath. He shifted inside her, and now she was the one to gasp as he stroked over her g-spot. Now that he had it, he held her in place, grinding and pushing, feeling how she tightened, how she panted.

He kept one arm locked around her waist while he slipped his free hand between her thighs. The tip of his finger found her clit. Rubbed it.

She keened. He thrust harder, his hips doing all the work as he remained buried inside her. Her own body gyrated, then stiffened as she came, her pussy squeezing him so tight.

He came. Hot spurts that reminded him of the fact that he'd once again forgotten a condom. He found it hard to care as they caught their breath, bodies entwined.

They finished showering in almost silence, cleansing each other, taking turns with the soap. His cock, while sated, remained semi-hard the entire time. It wouldn't take much for him to go again. He'd hadn't been this randy since his teen years.

Emerging into the bedroom, she went for the pile of clothes on a chair.

He flopped onto the bed to watch as she bent over to pull on underpants. "So now that I've passed the test, and you trust me, what's next?"

"Since we already took care of the fucking, now it's time to get our day going."

"I was talking about us. What's next for us?"

"There is no us. This is as far as it goes."

"What if I want more than just sex?"

"Are you really going to make this complicated?" She rolled her eyes. "Why can't it just be fucking? I told you I don't do boyfriends."

"Then it's time you changed that rule."

Her nose wrinkled. "Are you saying you actually want to date me? What are we, in high school?"

"Date. Fuck. Be with. Protect."

"I don't need some knight in shining armor. I can save myself."

"I am sure you can, but would it kill you to have some help?"

"Maybe." Her lips twitched. "If I let you be my boyfriend, does that mean you'll buy me dinner?"

"Probably. And take you to the movies."

"You planning to visit often from Pasadena?"

Apparently, she hadn't forgotten that he was here on a temporary gig. "I'm not married to my job if that's what you're asking. Relocation is an option."

"I don't want you making that kind of commitment. We might get tired of each other in a few days."

"Or you might discover you can't stand to live without me."

She snorted. "Doubtful. But I like your optimism. You think you like me now, but let's see how you do once you get to know the real me."

"So long as the real you doesn't resort to any more mickeys, I'm pretty sure I can handle it. And by the way, as your boyfriend, that means you can ask me shit, and I'll do my best to be honest."

"Only your best?"

"There are some things, like my past military career, that I can't talk about. Jobs I've done where I signed a confidentiality contract."

"I can handle that. So long as you respect the fact I have some things I can't talk about either. KM would cut me off from the tit if they thought I gave away too many secrets. I'm only talking to you because Mother said I could."

"You told your mother about me?" For some reason, that pleased him inordinately.

"Mother's known about you for a while. She thinks you're interesting, and she says if trusting you turns out to be a bad move, then I should eliminate you."

That quelled some of his warmth. "Speaking of people who know about me, where are your friends? Digging up more secrets?"

"Possibly. I know Tanya was going to see if she could get more info. She was right miffed at how much of your service record she couldn't read. Must be impressive given how much of it is blacked out."

"She'll be in big trouble if caught." The military didn't like its secrets being breached.

"Don't worry about T. She is the very best."

"Must be nice to have friends you can turn to when in need of accomplices to commit a crime." Said with a dry wryness.

"What crime?"

At his pointed stare, she smiled. Then laughed.

It was more than a man could bear. He rolled off the bed and dove on her. She squealed as he grabbed her by the wrists and pinned her arms over her head while his body smothered hers.

"What am I going to do with you?" he growled.

Shining eyes met his. "Do me."

A good plan. Philip kissed her and planned to do more but a rapid knock and yelled "Breakfast!" ruined his plans.

"Oooh, I could go for some food," she exclaimed.

"I'd rather eat in bed," he grumbled. Might be less chance of being drugged.

She nipped his chin. "We don't have time for another round. We've got work to do today."

"Work? What work? It's Saturday." And the big game wasn't until Sunday afternoon.

She twisted out of reach, and her panty-clad ass taunted as she bent to grab some clothes off a chair. His shirt and pants hit him in the face, and by the time he extricated himself, she was heading out the door, dressed in shorts and a tank top. He hurried to catch up, forgoing his shoes and padding down the stairs only to stop at the bottom at the sight of plywood screwed over the living room window.

"What the hell happened?" Philip said aloud.

"Some asshat tossed a brick through it. The glass guy will be by around ten to fix it."

The woman's reply had him turning to see the redhead from the night before. "Who threw it?"

"More than likely Pedro or one of his cronies. Trying to psych Carla out."

Given Philip had just seen her, it didn't seem to have worked. "You're Meredith, right?" He couldn't be sure he entirely trusted his memories of the night before given the drug.

She winked. "Any guy that Carla lets sleep in her bed can call me Merry."

"Who says he slept?" Carla yelled from the kitchen. "Or did you not hear the headboard knocking before we came down?

"TMI!" hollered Tanya from somewhere on the

main floor. "I don't need to know about your freaky sex life."

"At least some of us have a sex life. You ever gonna get over what's his name?" Carla taunted.

"His name was Tommy, and he was the love of my life," Tanya could be heard huffing.

"He was your first and only boyfriend, who knocked you up as a teenager and left before he even knew he was gonna be a daddy."

"And? He was my soulmate."

"It's been eleven years, T. Get laid," Carla snapped.

"No, thank you," was the pert reply.

"Do they argue like this often?" Philip asked Meredith as he followed her into the kitchen.

"All the time, just like sisters," Meredith said fondly. "And if you call me their mother, I'll slap you."

"No one is like Mother," the trio of women exclaimed then giggled, leaving him at a total loss.

Breakfast proved an interesting experience with him seated across from Carla, his plate piled high with hash browns, toast, eggs, and sausage.

No one said a word about the previous night, although there was much teasing about the fact that Carla had invited a man to their group.

Only once breakfast was finished did things turn serious.

Tanya brought out the laptop, an innocuous-looking, battered Dell that thumped on the table. She tapped as she began talking.

"No hits on any of the boards I posted on. If anyone's seen Pedro, then they're keeping quiet."

Carla, hands full of dirty dishes and headed to the sink, tossed over her shoulder, "I don't think he's been out of jail too long. My guess is he's hiding because he breached his bail conditions."

"He's obviously made new friends, though, given he's been tailing you and was involved in the drive-by."

Philip blinked as the information was tossed around, then slammed his hands on the table. "Hold on just a fucking second. You didn't tell me he was behind the shooting."

"He's also been following me, tried to snag Nico at his school, and is probably the one behind my tires being slashed and the brick last night."

"This is serious shit. You need to call the cops."

The women passed a knowing glance amongst each other before Meredith snorted. "The cops, really? What are they going to do exactly?"

"Arrest him."

"For what, being a jerk?" Carla asked sarcastically. "None of the stuff can be proven. He'll have an alibi and claim I'm making shit up. And even if they did arrest him, he'd be back on the streets in twenty-four hours. Maybe less. Gunning for me and Nico."

"So, what are you suggesting? You going to kill him?"

Dead silence.

He frowned. "Carla..." Killing was serious business. It fucked with a person's mind. She shouldn't even joke about going down that path.

She laughed. "Had you going, didn't I?"

The women snickered.

He didn't entirely relax. "What is your plan then?" Because he wasn't entirely convinced. He'd seen the guns.

"First, we need to locate him," Tanya said, tapping on her laptop.

"Then, we take care of him," was Carla's ominous statement.

"She means we'll call the cops." Meredith waggled her phone.

"I thought you said they wouldn't do shit?" He was so fucking confused.

"They might not be able to do much, but if he's broken probation, then that might get him tossed in the clink for a while longer. Long enough for Carla and Nico to start over somewhere," Meredith explained.

He scrubbed his face. "It's a crazy plan. I don't see how you figure you'll find him. And what if you do? Then what? By the sounds of it, he will get violent."

"I know how to protect myself," Carla said. "We all do."

"Against guns? Gangbangers?" He shook his head. "It's nuts. You'll get hurt." He had to find a way to handle this for her.

"We can't exactly do nothing," Carla remarked.

"You're right. Which is why I'm going to take care of this asshole."

"Ah, look at that. Carla's new beau wants to keep her safe. How cute," Meredith chortled.

Carla laughed. "What are you going to do?"

"You're not the only one with a gun."

Tanya clasped her hands. "Oooh, he really is perfect for her."

"Question is, does he know how to use it?"

The words made sense, yet he got a feeling he'd missed some kind of joke. Especially given that both Tanya and Carla snickered.

"Three times." Carla held up her fingers.

His cheeks heated. So the sexual innuendo was intentional. "I'll handle this Pedro character."

"While the little women stay tucked inside where it's safe?" Meredith stated in a high-pitched, girly voice. It dropped an octave. "Like hell, sugar. We are all going."

Carla snapped her fingers. "We're wasting time. Everyone is going. T and Merry, you stick together. I'll keep an eye on Philip. Keep him from getting in trouble."

"Excuse me?" he blustered.

Meredith and Tanya left the kitchen with the blonde muttering, "Uh-oh, lover's spat."

Philip found himself alone with Carla.

She patted his cheek. "Sorry, soldier, I'm sure you

think you're capable of handling Pedro, but given it's been a while since you were in the army, you might be a little rusty."

"I'm not rusty." He sighed. "And you're not going to stay here are you."

"Nope. So don't even bother trying, or we won't be getting naked together later."

"Where are we starting the search?"

"Bars, but most don't open for hours. So, we're going to check in on my son first."

"Where is Nico?"

"He's at my aunt Judy's with Portia and the girls."

"Are you sure this Pedro character doesn't know where she lives?" He'd hate to think that something might happen to the boy.

"I was careful dropping him off, and even if Pedro dared to show his face, Auntie would handle it. She hates bullies."

Hating bullies was all fine and dandy, but he had an issue with letting an old woman deal with a thug. Not to mention, he didn't want anyone scaring or harming Nico. He liked the kid. A lot. The mother, too. Despite the fact that she appeared determined to drive him batty.

Philip followed her pert ass as it went swinging out of the room. It wiggled all the way up the stairs, a siren's call he couldn't resist.

He closed the bedroom door behind them. "I really wish you'd let me handle this Pedro guy alone."

"Don't be silly. I've got my big, strong man to protect me. And my magnum." She smirked as she dressed, the holster built into her jean jacket. It made him wish he had access to more of his wardrobe. The good news was that he could now openly wear the gun he'd stashed in the trunk of his car.

When they went outside, and he retrieved it, she admired it. "A Sauer. Good weapon. I have one in a locker at the Atlanta airport."

"Because?"

"It's a nexus location on many of my flights."

"You travel?"

"Not too often, but enough I have a few stashes."

For some reason, that made him grin and shake his head. "Me, too. Although, my airport locker is in Chicago."

"They have the best public toilets and deep-dish pizza." As they neared his car parked on the road, she held out her hand. "Keys."

He snorted. "I'm driving."

"I know where we're going."

"Why can't you just give me directions."

"Because I want to make sure no one is following."

"I am perfectly capable of ensuring we don't have a tail. This happens to be something I do on a regular basis." Oliveira was paranoid, and so was Philip.

Carla perused him for a moment. "Fine. You drive, but if we get chased, you'd better hold the car steady, so I can shoot out their tires from a window."

"Why not just get on the hood and surf it so that you can leap into their vehicle and overpower them?"

"That trick doesn't work so good outside movies. Bullets, though"—she tapped her hidden gun—"they stop bad guys dead." She grinned.

He shook his head. This playful Carla took getting used to, but her sarcastic humor was fun. Especially since she seemed serious about it.

What if she really were as deadly as she claimed?

I might just have to marry her. A thought that didn't bring panic.

Philip took a circuitous route to Aunt Judy's place, doubling back and weaving, not using signals before taking sudden turns. Even the sharpest ones didn't elicit screams of fear but rather excitement. Carla squealed as she held on to the oh-shit bar. She laughed, as well. "Go, soldier, go. Faster."

She was nuts.

And he loved it.

He pulled up in front of a rather nice home in a suburban area with green lawns, empty driveways, and most windows framed in curtains not covered by vertical blinds.

The door immediately opened, and Nico flew out, arms flailing, legs pumping. "Mami!"

Carla spilled out of the car and held her arms open wide. Her son flew into them as Philip emerged from the car. Given everything he'd learned, now he was the one staring all around, looking for a vehicle that was out of place. Because in that moment, he knew for a fact that he wanted them safe. Happy.

Wanted to be a part of that close family.

A woman appeared in the door flanked by matching girls. Obviously, twins, both in pink rompers. They held back until their mother said, "Go and say hi to Auntie Carla."

Nico got out of the way just in time and made his way over to Philip. "Hey, Coach, what you doing with my mom?"

It shouldn't have made Philip blush, yet it did. Thankfully, the strange woman saved him. "You must be Philip Moore. I've heard so much about you."

He shook the extended hand and wondered what she'd heard. Before he could ask, a gray-haired woman with a steely gaze appeared. "We should take this conversation inside."

Entering the house, the door shut behind them and hissed as if pressurized. Philip glanced behind him and noticed the door clicking as it locked.

Heavy-duty safety features. With an arm around her son, Carla led him into the living room along with the others. The polished wood floors went well with the brocade couch and matching armchairs. Everything appeared pristine and only missed plastic covers.

"Nico, can you and the girls empty the dishwasher please?"

"Yes, Aunt Judy." The children didn't even argue before vacating the room.

"Sit," Aunt Judy with the steely gaze ordered.

He sat, and Carla joined him on the couch.

"I'm Judy. This is Portia." She waved to the woman who resembled the little girls. "And you're the soldier?" She eyed him up and down. "Seems in decent enough shape."

"Nothing wrong with his body," Carla said.

"Can he use it?"

Expecting another innuendo, he spoke first. "He uses it just fine, thank you."

Carla smirked. "Actually, I haven't had a chance to test him in hand-to-hand combat. But he is energetic. He also carries a gun."

Judy sniffed. "Everyone and their mother has a gun these days. Question is, will he know when to use it or panic and shoot his own team?"

"I don't panic if that's what you're asking," Philip said. "And I avoid shooting when possible."

"Squeamish?"

"More like I'd rather not answer questions I don't have to." Why did he shoot? Did he feel threatened? Was there a personal connection between him and the victim? Last time he'd shot a mugger to protect himself, it had taken weeks before the cops stopped harassing him.

"Did Tanya find anything?" Judy asked.

"Hold on a second. Are we just talking in front of him?" Portia asked. "Has he been given clearance?"

"Mother approved it."

"Did Mother say why?"

Carla shrugged. "You know how she is. She doesn't always give us a reason. Just orders."

"And we listen," Portia said with a frown, still staring at him.

"You guys are sisters?" he said, trying to follow their conversation.

Portia replied, "We are tighter than blood. Can we trust you?"

"I would never do anything to hurt Carla or Nico." The truth.

"Fine." Portia turned away and rummaged in a purse. "For Pedro, I've got a sedative you can use if you get close to him. Also, one more dose of the TTT43 in case you want him to confess to the cops. If you can't eliminate him due to witnesses, then see if you can drop the teal one into a drink. It will cause a massive cardiac arrest…"

"More drugs?" Philip said dryly as Portia handed over three plastic bags, each with a pill inside.

"Useful if we get close enough, but more than likely, things will get rough," Carla admitted.

"Which is why you should let the pros handle it," Philip reiterated.

"The cops aren't pros. And you don't have to come if you're scared."

"Not scared, just not stupid. You're hunting a known criminal. You can't expect him to follow any rules."

"I don't have a problem with breaking the rules. You ready, soldier?"

As he'd ever be.

Because more than ever, he wanted to know who the real Carla was? Did she have what it took to go after a thug?

What if it came down to a life-or-death situation? Could she act?

The first kill was hard. For some, too hard.

If he could prevent it, Philip would make sure she never had to make that choice.

CHAPTER EIGHTEEN

PHILIP STUCK CLOSE to Carla as they hit the bars near the neighborhood most likely to host Pedro. A guy like him would want to be surrounded by folks who believed in keeping their mouths shut when cops showed up. A place that didn't see any problem with stealing from the rich—or the middle class. That believed the drug trade was just another commerce.

"I think I'm overdressed," Philip muttered after they'd entered the first tavern. Business was sluggish given it was midafternoon. Hours still until the true crowd arrived.

Carla stifled a chuckle. At least now, Philip better understood her outfit of torn jeans, faded, snug T-shirt, and hair left unbound. She fit right in this neighborhood with her foul mouth and sassy attitude, whereas he, with his slacks and collared polo shirt, did not.

The side-eyed glances angled his way didn't deter

him. Nor did the muttered insults, not all of them in English.

Philip didn't seem to care. He stood tall. Wide. Over the counters in the bars, in the large mirrors, she could see his menacing countenance.

Kind of sexy. Also, very annoying.

He made it hard to get any replies. People froze at the sight of him, his military bearing reminiscent of law enforcement.

All this to say, people weren't talking around him. Still, she didn't need actual verbal confirmation of Pedro's patronage. A flicker of the eyes, a too convincing, "Never seen him," was enough for her to spot the liar.

No surprise, the tavern that hosted Pedro was Mexican in nature, offering authentic cuisine and tequila from bottles holding a worm.

"Well, if you do see him, tell him Carlotta's looking for him." She felt more than heard Philip's disapproval. He'd given her hell the first time she'd done it.

"Are you trying to make yourself a target?" he'd hissed when they exited that first bar.

"I don't have time to wait for Pedro to make his next move. This will hopefully flush him out."

Or she'd corner him later tonight after he'd drunk a few. Given that was probably a few hours away, she'd driven them a block away to a motel she'd seen. The kind that rented by the hour.

She paid cash for a room and dragged Philip to the

third floor. He eyed the bed. "Think they ever wash these sheets."

The disgust made her snicker. "Probably not. Come here." He joined her at the window and then whistled. "Is it me, or does this room give us a perfect vantage point over the bar?"

"At least from the west side. We can spot him coming."

"So long as he enters through the front."

She shrugged. "True. Which is why we'll be paying another visit around tenish."

"Which is hours from now."

"Oh my, whatever will we do while we wait?"

"We won't be using that bed. I'd rather not need shots later."

A laugh escaped her. "I wouldn't have taken you for such a princess. I thought soldiers could handle any conditions."

He straddled her body, pinning her against the window where her ass sat on the old heating/cooling unit. "Are you calling me a pussy?"

She grabbed hold of his shirt and yanked him down. "Are you really going to pass up a chance to bang me because of some dirty sheets?"

"I already said, we don't need a bed." He palmed her ass and lifted her. "But someone needs to keep watch." He spun her around so she faced the window. His hands were at her waist, pulling at her jeans, tugging them down.

She didn't stop him. She knew no one could see them. Not only were they high enough but the outside glare also kept anyone from seeing in.

His hand slipped between her legs. Stroking. Touching. Making her wet.

Oh, so wet.

When his tongue followed, she might have closed her eyes rather than watch the street. She couldn't help herself as he licked her. Brought her pleasure just by using his tongue. When he added his fingers to the mix, she moaned and thrust out her bottom. Pushed against his digits, begged for more.

When she came, she didn't hold it in. She screamed. Loudly. Not caring if anyone heard. He slid into her, the hard length of him teasing her still-throbbing flesh. He moved inside her, stroked her, revived her fading orgasm, his finger finding the nub of her clit and rubbing.

Stroking.

Stringing her higher and higher until she came again. Harder this time. Her screams more like short, loud barks of bliss.

He remained folded over her for a while after. Holding her. And she loved it.

Loved—

She abruptly straightened and shoved him away. "I should get cleaned up before I got to run out of here with cum running down my leg. Which, by the way, wouldn't happen if you'd use a condom." Good thing she was on the pill.

"I'm clean," he announced as she entered a bathroom that wasn't as gross as expected. The water at least ran clean, and while she didn't trust the dingy towel, she wiped herself and splashed water on her face.

Spent moment staring. *What am I doing?*

Falling for him, obviously.

Was that such a bad thing?

Probably, because she got the impression he still didn't take her hints about who and what she was seriously. He still thought it all a joke. That she played at being a tough-ass killer.

When he found out the truth...would she have to eliminate him? She wasn't sure she could.

Hell, she'd not even wanted to let him in on her secret, but her sisters and Mother had convinced her to give him a try. If things didn't work out, well, she at least knew where to bury the body.

But what if things did work? In a sense, that frightened her more.

Exiting the bathroom, Philip had his back to her as he stared out the window. "No sign of a big, bald dude yet."

"It's early still." Early being the twilight before true nightfall. While Pedro might have come to threaten in the daytime, she got the impression that he usually stalked at night. Cowards preferred the cover of darkness to hide.

Shadows wouldn't be enough to save him once she found him.

"Tell me about Matias," Philip said, the sudden query startling.

"There's nothing to say."

"He's the father of your child."

"The only good thing he ever did."

"So why get with him if he was such a shit?" Philip asked, turning to face her.

"It wasn't so much my choice as just something that happened. He saw me. He wanted me. He had me." She shrugged. The elation at having the baddest boy in the neighborhood interested didn't last long once she realized what kind of man he was—and wasn't.

"Did you leave him?"

"Yeah." Then, because he might as well know the entire ugly truth. "He killed my family because of it."

"What?" His words emerged low.

"My mother. Two brothers. Shot. In our apartment. Then the friend who shielded me was next."

"Geezus, Carla. I'm sorry."

"Why? It's not your fault I made a shitty choice in life. The only good that came of it was Nico. And after Matias killed my family, I was terrified I'd lose my son. Luckily, I made a new friend who helped me escape before anything else could happen."

"You said Matias died?"

"He did."

"Good."

"Why?" she asked.

"Because, otherwise, I'd have to kill him."

She could see by his expression that he meant it. She reached out to cup his cheek. "That is sweet. But I handled it myself."

"What's that mean?"

Rather than reply, Carla pointed out the window. "There's the motherfucker." Pedro's bald pate proved noticeable among his friends as they sauntered up the sidewalk. The car at the curb was the same one used in the drive-by.

There was no more time for talking as they exited the room. Only as they reached the sidewalk did Philip say, "Where are you going?"

"To see Pedro."

"I thought the plan was to call the cops."

"Change of plans." She hastened her step.

"Carla!"

She didn't slow, and in moments, she was inside the bar. It proved much busier than before. The press of bodies making it tough, especially given her stature, to spot Pedro in the mix.

The hand on her ass didn't belong to Philip—too small—and as Carla turned, she only had a brief glimpse of white teeth in a dark face before the guy was wrenched away.

Philip got in the dude's face and snarled, "Hands to yourself, asshole." He shoved the young guy, who stumbled hard against a table.

The jealous streak was cute but misplaced as silence descended.

"Hey, gringo, you think you're so tough picking on my little brother?" The guy who spoke wasn't exactly huge by any means; however, he had a few friends at his back.

Philip gave them all a cool smile. "Maybe your brother should try respecting women if he doesn't want to get schooled."

"I'm going to fuck up that pretty face of yours, asshole," the guy spat. Carla inched out of the way, not really wanting to get involved, especially since she caught a glimpse of a bald head. She stood on tiptoe and caught sight of Pedro leaning over the bar, talking to the guy behind it.

Eyes suddenly veered her way. Pedro saw her. Smirked. Gave her the finger.

Fucker. Carla tried to squeeze between a pair of bodies, only they were intent on the fight developing at her back. A skirmish started by a jealous Philip.

I should have left him with Aunt Judy.

A glance over her shoulder showed the situation getting worse. Philip and the guy he'd pissed off stood toe-to-toe. Which meant, Philip didn't see the other fellow sneaking up.

"Behind you!"

Too late.

The chair smashed into Philip's back, and she winced. That had to hurt. However, it didn't stop Philip from whirling and swinging. His fist connected, and while she didn't hear the crack over hoots and hollers of excitement, she could imagine it. Training had taught her not to cringe at the sound of bones breaking and flesh getting pummeled.

It seemed Philip knew how to hide pain since he didn't even grimace at the agony he surely must be in. A spot in front of her opened as the crowd shifted, and she eyed it. Then behind her at Philip again. Things were getting worse. The concept of a fair fight totally went out the window as about four guys threw themselves at Philip. He didn't let that daunt him, his fists moved quickly, his body ducking and absorbing blows.

He was good, but numbers would prevail.

I'd better help him. Flipping around, she shoved her way through the gap between two bodies and joined the fray. Her small, lithe frame allowed her to slip in between opponents where her well-placed elbow jabs, foot stomps, and knees to the balls had men gasping and stumbling. Her aid gave Philip some breathing room, and with a shot to the face that would probably result in nose surgery, he laid out the fellow he'd started the fight with.

It didn't stop the brawl, but the good news? The focus was no longer entirely on Philip. She grabbed him by the hand and pulled him out of there, emerging into the cooler evening air. The door swung shut behind them, cutting off most of the chaotic battle.

They kept moving, Carla still holding Philip's hand as she made it to the corner and turned into the alley.

"Where are you taking me? The car is the other way."

"While you were playing my dick is bigger than yours, Pedro slipped out the back."

"Shit. Sorry."

"Don't be too sorry. At least I learned one thing." Philip had a little psycho in him given his jealousy issues. She also realized she wasn't bothered by it. It only made him sexier. But she didn't say that aloud. Instead, she went with, "You aren't a half-bad fighter."

"Says the woman who was taking out guys twice her size."

"If we'd had more time, I would have made them cry for their mothers."

He shook his head as they jogged the length of the alley. No one in sight. "Where did you learn to fight?"

In a grassy field where she'd enjoyed the taste of dirt the first few months of training. Then, she got better.

In the winter, they moved indoors to the wooden floor of the old converted gymnasium. The academy ran out of an old school situated on several acres of land. Remote and perfect for a training camp.

Given they weren't exactly in a private place or

with time to spare, she kept it to the short version. "A girl should know how to protect herself."

"I think we missed Pedro." Reaching the far end of the alley that joined with a small residential street, the only thing moving was distant taillights.

"Yeah, but now he knows I'm looking."

"So, he's going to hide."

She snorted. "Please. A guy like him? Pedro ain't going to hide. He's gonna have to do something to get his balls back. All his buddies know he ran from a woman."

Philip stared at her. "You made yourself a target."

"I already was a target. I just waved a red flag."

"Hoping Pedro would be dumb and just charge you." Philip sighed and rubbed his face. "You never intended to call the cops, did you?"

Her lips twitched. "Will you spank me if I say no?"

"I'll spank you no matter what," he growled.

And she just might let him.

The door behind them opened, spilling light and noise. Someone yelled, "Out here. I think I see them."

She tugged at Philip's hand. "We should go."

They ran the few blocks to his car, and this time, when she held out her hand for the keys, he didn't argue.

She drove like a bat out of hell with gangbangers on her tail. She went straight home because the whole point of poking Pedro was to get him to do something stupid. Like attack her on familiar and protected turf.

She parked Philip's car on the street, across from her place. "Probably safer here," she noted.

"You think they'll hit tonight."

"I'm counting on it." Entering her place, she whipped out her phone and opened an app with a house in a locked box. She began tapping icons.

"What are you doing?" he asked.

"Arming the house."

Given it was a townhouse, she only had to worry about frontal and rear attacks.

From the back, anyone sneaking would have to climb a fence lined with an electrical current.

Anyone not wearing insulated gloves would be drooling and pissing their pants on the ground.

If they made it to the yard, she had motion sensors. No booby traps. It wasn't safe with Nico and his friends sometimes playing back there.

All the windows and doors were equipped with alarms. Each one a different pitch to indicate what section of the house was breached. Her roof—which Pedro probably wouldn't think of—had a motion and sound detection camera. No one was getting inside without her knowing it.

"Take off your shirt," she said once everything activated.

"Is now the time, considering everything?" he asked.

"Now is the best time. Or are you worried we'll be underpowered? Does this make you feel better?" She dropped to her knees and rummaged under the couch. Her fingers caught the Velcro seam of the fabric. Tugged it free. She reached inside the opening and closed her fingers around a barrel. She lay the assault rifle she pulled from under the couch on the living room table. Dumping out a vase with plastic flowers, she pulled out a false foam layer, then a few extra cartridges. She waved at the pile. "There. How about now? Feeling reassured?"

"Not exactly. Where do you hide the flamethrower?"

"Attic. I also keep my mini Gatling up there."

"The sad part is I believe you."

"I like being prepared. So, strip off that shirt." She left the room on that order, returning with a first aid kit and a bag of frozen veggies.

"I don't think a bandage will help," he noted.

Carla eyed him. The bruises on his ribs were already ripening. Still, the cold would soothe. She tossed him the veggies. "Sit down and hold the package to it."

"I'll be fine."

"Sit. Down." She took a menacing step towards him.

"You can't make me," he stated.

She proved him wrong. Her foot hooked around his ankle, and her shove unbalanced him. Philip hit the couch with a wince.

"Was that necessary?"

"Yes." She straddled his lap and grabbed his chin. Tilting his face left and right. "You took a few good shots. But you're still pretty. Any loose teeth?"

"They're solid. What about you? Did you get hit?"

A faint smile pulled at her mouth. "Some of us know better than to stand in front of a fist."

"Smartass."

"Very. This might sting." She held up a bottle she'd pulled from the first aid kit. Brown glass with a white lid. No label.

"What is that?"

"Something that doesn't exist yet."

"But you happen to have it."

"You might want to bite down on something." She dabbed him with the wet brush on the end of the lid. The ochre fluid smeared across the bruise under his eye.

He blinked. Stiffened—his body, not his cock. His jaw locked.

"Does it hurt?" she teased as she layered more of the goop on his ribs where the swelling appeared most intense.

"It's fine."

She highly doubted it. Having used the rapid healing formula before, she knew how much it stung. The man didn't show it other than a tenseness in his limbs and features.

Sexy. Philip was one tough bastard.

She dropped a kiss on his lips and went to move,

only his hands grabbed her around the waist. Kept her sitting on his lap.

"Where do you think you're going?"

"To check on the perimeter."

"I thought you had alarms for that."

"I do."

"It's my turn to check you over," he remarked.

"I told you I wasn't hurt."

"Then this won't take long." He cupped her face but rather than tilt it around for a better look, he dropped a light kiss on her forehead, her nose, each cheek, her lips.

Then he nibbled the tip of her chin, which brought a giggle. A sigh slipped free as his lips explored her neck, the lobe of her ear, the collarbone peeking from her shirt.

"Find anything yet?" she asked as his hands skimmed under the hem of her shirt.

"Still looking," Philip murmured, dipping her back, exposing the tan line of her belly. He leaned forward and kissed it. Close enough to give her pussy a happy jolt.

Unfortunately, he didn't go any further. His phone rang. A shrill, old style *brrring-brrring*.

"Ignore it," she ordered, wiggling on his lap.

"I shouldn't. It's Oliveira."

Why would he be calling this late? "Answer it."

Hearing only one side of the conversation didn't stop her from grasping the gist.

"No, she hasn't changed her mind." Philip paused. "She has a life here with the boy." A frown. "Why are you trying to force the issue? She has no interest in the academy." Another moment of silence as he listened. "Nico's not been home in two days? That is odd. Maybe he's visiting some friends."

Her brow rose. Oliveira was having her son watched? And not by Philip. What the hell was the man's obsession?

"I'll let her know you need to speak to her when I see her." Philip hung up and tossed the phone onto the coffee table. "He wants you to call him."

She rolled her eyes as she straddled his body. "I'll just bet he does. Who the fuck does he think he is, having me watched?"

"Obviously not watched too well given he had no idea I was here with you."

"The fact he employs half-assed idiots—"

"Hey!"

"Why is he so determined? Nico is not joining his school."

"Would it be so bad?" Philip asked.

"I am not moving to Pasadena."

"What if I move out here?"

She snared the veggies melting on the couch and left him, using the time to put them into the freezer to digest what he said.

Was he seriously contemplating moving here? For her?

The excitement almost got buried by the panic. It was too much. Too soon. Too serious.

They'd only just met. And yes, the sex was good, but good enough to actually commit to a relationship?

"You ran away rather than answer." He cornered her in the kitchen, still shirtless.

"I don't think you should move."

"And I'm not into long-distance commuting. If I'm going to be your boyfriend—"

"I never said you were."

"I am." He didn't ask. Simply stated.

She chose not to argue. "Where would you stay? Because you can't stay here."

"Because of Nico. I know. I'll rent a place. Close by so I can sneak over every night."

"Every? What if I don't want sex every day? Maybe some nights I'll want to watch television or dive into a book."

"Then we'll snuggle and watch the boob tube. I'll play Angry Birds while you read."

"You have an answer for everything."

He shrugged. "What can I say. I'm a smart guy. A guy who wants to see where this is going." He bracketed her with his arms, keeping her pressed to the fridge.

"I'm not who you think I am."

"So I'm beginning to discover." He slid his mouth over hers. "But the good news is, I can handle more than you think." His hand slid under her shirt, cupping her breast.

She whispered her next words against his mouth. "You better be right, soldier." Because she liked him. Liked him a lot. And it seemed he reciprocated, but he had yet to learn what she was truly capable of.

What if he couldn't handle it? She'd have to disappear or kill him.

Problem was, she didn't think she could do the latter.

She cupped his face and drew him closer for a kiss. While she couldn't put into words the things he made her feel, she could show him.

And she did. Hiking her leg around his hip. Gasping when he entered her.

Filled her.

When the climax ebbed, she leaned into him. Basking in the closeness. Softening.

She couldn't be soft now.

Carla pushed away from him. "I should check on Nico."

Everything appeared quiet. Aunt Judy claimed that no one had so much as looked at her place. None of her alarms sounded.

They passed the night in peace. So peaceful, she awoke at one point, drooling in Philip's lap on the couch.

Since she was already down there, she said good morning to his cock. He crowed with the dawn.

It was only over breakfast that he broached the subject of the day's plan.

"Think he'll return to the bar later today?" he asked in between bites of his peanut butter toast.

"Hopefully. If not, I'm sure he'll poke his head up soon."

"How you going to explain to Nico why he can't play today?"

"I'm not. He's playing."

"You can't be serious," Philip exclaimed. "Pedro might make a move during the game."

"Doubtful, given there will be witnesses."

"You're taking a chance."

True. Yet what other choice did she have? Nico couldn't stay at Aunt Judy's forever. Just like running might not solve anything.

Best to face it here and now. On her terms.

She dropped a kiss on Philip's lips, tasting the peanut butter. "Don't worry. Me and my sisters already have a plan."

"I feel like those words need ominous music," he declared.

"Don't worry, soldier. I've got this." She patted his cheek. He dragged her into his lap.

They were a few minutes late leaving to grab Nico. But she didn't mind. If things didn't work out, then it might be the last time.

CHAPTER NINETEEN

CARLA HAD A PLAN, and she wouldn't tell Philip about it. Just said not to worry. "Coach the game," she'd said with a smile. She'd handle the rest.

Emasculating and hot all at once. Philip found it fascinating that she didn't seem afraid. Rather coldly determined. Carla wasn't one to back down. She saw a threat and faced it head-on.

He loved that about her, even as it frightened him. Now that he'd found her, he didn't want to lose her, not to some asshole with a grudge.

Which was why, despite the warm weather, he wore his coaching jacket—a bulky thing that hid his holster and gun. Most of the time, he didn't feel a need to wear a weapon. Guns should always be a last resort.

Carla, on the other hand, seemed to feel differently. She wore a holster under her sweatshirt. Another strapped to her ankle, her bootcut jeans hiding it. She even had a knife strapped to one wrist.

"You're packing to kill," he noted as they dressed in the bedroom.

"Wounded beasts are the most dangerous."

"You can't start shooting in a crowd of people."

"Don't worry. This isn't my first rodeo." She patted his cheek, which wasn't reassuring.

She wouldn't let them leave via the front door. "There's a car parked three houses up. I am pretty sure there's someone in it watching."

"Oliveira's spy? Or Pedro?"

"Don't know.

"Shouldn't we find out?"

"How?" she asked. "Gonna walk out the door, up to their car, and tap on their window? Do you really think they'll wait patiently and answer your questions?"

"They might."

She snorted. "Stop arguing and haul your cute butt over my fence."

Just to be ornery, he knelt and offered her a hand over. She glared as she grabbed the lip and pulled herself up.

He quickly followed. They met up with Tanya two streets over, her rental spacious enough for the three of them and the equipment in the back seat.

"You rob a computer store?" he asked, noting the three laptops as well as the giant mesh ear for listening.

"Borrowed so I could keep eyes on a few locations at once."

Apparently, Carla wasn't sticking with him. She and Tanya dropped him early at the soccer field.

"Where are you going?" he asked, leaning in the car window.

"Fetching Nico for the game."

"Be careful." He knew better than to insist on going with her. Besides, it wouldn't hurt if he took a moment to check out the field and the school buildings.

"Careful is for pussies."

"Pussies tend to not need stitches or gravestones."

"I want to be cremated." She hauled him close and kissed him. "It will be all right."

"It better," he grumbled.

"Oh, and don't take it personal if I scream about your coaching skills during the game," she said with a final smirk.

Then she was gone. He spent the next hour getting acquainted with the school and the field. Made note of the cars parked. The random foot traffic. He also noted that he wasn't the only one to get there before game time.

A shiny Mercedes—with the vanity plate *Cougar*—was parked close to the field. Same one he'd seen that night outside Carla's place before they drugged him. So, Meredith was here. Did she have a car full of spying laptops like Tanya? Or was she armed to the gills like Carla?

It was crazy to even think something would happen today. There would be a crowd of people. Witnesses. Surely, Pedro wouldn't be stupid enough to try something.

Then again, if Philip believed that, why did he wear a gun?

As the first of the boys arrived, Philip remained alert and put Pedro to the back of his mind. The team arrived in trickles and were soon warming up, excited and nervous about the big game. The bleachers filled, and when those were full, people pulled out lawn chairs—the fold-up versions that swallowed bodies and had a cupholder for the truly prepared. He was sure some of those thermoses held coffee, but he'd wager that more than a few had a little something extra.

The day proved perfect for playing. The grass was lush and green, the lines freshly painted. The nets had been patched of holes, ready for some epic kicks.

The kids were bundles of energy. Ready and raring to go. This was what they'd trained for all year.

When the game finally started, they shone on the field. While Philip might only have come on board for the last week, he was mightily impressed with them, and his voice rang out as one of encouragement. Even when they faltered, he was there to bolster them. When they scored, he yelled as loudly as he could.

Nico shone brighter than all the other stars. The boy moved quickly, with a sixth sense of where to go. When to kick.

The game was neck and neck at the end of the second period, neither team ready to give up. They fought hard, their bodies damp with sweat and their faces flushed with exertion. The crowd hushed as the ball was carried back and forth. Going to the goal. Stolen, headed the other way. Stopped. And it went on.

The last minute on the scoreboard flipped to seconds and began counting down. Nico had the ball. He was carrying it downfield, his stamina outpacing the rest of the boys.

The boy wound up. His leg pulled back, but rather than watch the result, Philip's attention was drawn to the roar of motorcycles. He turned his head and saw a stream of them arriving on the street closest to the field. Spilling into the parking lot.

There were screams behind him. He flipped quickly, looking for carnage, only to realize Nico had done it. He'd won the game.

The boys celebrated on the field as did the crowd at first until a few noticed the revving of engines. Heads turned.

The happy dances on the field slowed and then halted.

Players and parents alike stared as men wearing leather and bandannas got off their bikes. A few more poured out of cars. Around a dozen or so thugs, some holding baseball bats, others with tire irons. A few even sported guns, which they fired into the air, the loud crack bringing forth more than a few panicked whispers and more screams.

Fergus was the one to brashly confront them. "What are you doing here? Get out of here. Take your shit elsewhere. There's kids around."

"Shut the fuck up, lardass." A tire iron was swung at Fergus, catching him in the arm, drawing a shrill scream.

Pandemonium erupted.

In the chaos, Philip saw Carla standing firm, looking pissed. As for Nico, Philip's gaze strayed to the boy, who stared in shock. He saw Tanya heading for Nico at a run.

"Nico. This way," Philip heard Tanya cry amidst the chaos. He waited to see the boy heading towards her at the far end of the field where there were no thugs before he turned back to the men threatening the crowd.

With this kind of violence erupting, he'd wager that more than one call had been made to the police, but how long before they arrived? Even two minutes could have dire consequences, especially since Carla wasn't moving with the crowd away from the thugs but towards them.

Idiot.

Philip waded against the crush of fleeing parents, some towing younger children along with them. Despite the urgency, he didn't dare draw his weapon, not yet. He waited until he cleared the bleachers and caught sight of Carla's ass as she stood against a mob of at least twelve guys. Some slapping bats and metal bars against their palms. All of them leering and hooting.

The biggest guy, standing slightly apart from them, sneered. It wasn't hard to figure out that he was their ringleader, Pedro.

And what did Carla do? She pulled a gun from under her sweatshirt and aimed it.

"I warned you, asshole. I said what would happen if you came near me again."

"You gonna shoot me?" Pedro mocked. He held out his arms. "I've got witnesses that will put your ass in jail and then guess who'll get custody of your boy. His loving uncle, Pedro."

"Like fuck will you get near my son. I'll see you dead first."

Philip didn't know if she would actually shoot Pedro in cold blood. A fellow to her left let out a yell and ran towards her, drawing her attention. Before Carla could fire, Philip pulled his own gun and shot the guy attacking her in the leg.

She cast a surprised glance over her shoulder. Bad mistake.

Pedro took advantage and lunged at her, his bulky frame slamming into Carla, taking her to the ground.

Fuck.

Especially since more than a few of Pedro's buddies turned to look at Philip. Including one with a gun.

If Philip shot him first, then he would have to move quickly to tag the guy on his—

"Oh, boys." A sultry Southern yodel had more than a few of the thugs turning their heads.

He wasn't the only one to do a double-take as Meredith, still dressed in crisp white slacks and a blouse, her red hair in an elegant upsweep, pointed a Taser and took the closest fellow out. The thug hit the ground, jiggling. With the Taser spent, she dropped it into her large purse, then smiled. "Who's next?"

A pair of men moved towards her, but Meredith didn't flee. The woman tapped her umbrella on the ground, and in a move straight from a movie, the parasol part of it fell away leaving only a stick.

Only.

Ha.

She wielded that thing with deadly accuracy, striking the surprised thugs in vulnerable areas that had them whimpering, yelping, and hitting the ground, holding their legs as she busted their knees, cradling their arms as she cracked a few bones.

Who the fuck were Carla's friends? *Interior designers, my ass.*

Philip spent a moment too long distracted because he never saw the fist that came out of nowhere to punch him.

"Fucker." He swung in retaliation, grunted when a heavy bar slammed into his back. His gun was useless in close quarters, but he didn't have a chance to tuck it away until he heard sirens.

Pedro's gang heard them too and scattered. The fight abruptly halted as they hauled ass and sped away, leaving only Meredith, who reattached the parasol to her stick with a jab at Philip, who hurriedly tucked his gun away, and...

Wait a second. Where the fuck was Carla?

CHAPTER TWENTY

GOOD THING CARLA wore running shoes because Pedro moved quickly once he realized he'd lost the upper hand. The coward bolted in the opposite direction of his buddies, leaving them to their fate.

Carla wasn't about to let him run free again. She took off after him, grimacing at the ache in her ribs. Could be there were a few that had cracked when that lumbering idiot crashed into her—which she blamed on Philip for distracting her.

The fucker actually used his gun. Carla might have gaped at Philip a moment too long as she got to see the true soldier at work.

Pedro made her pay for gawking. She hit the ground and lost her weapon, the jolt opening her fingers and sending it flying.

Shit.

Bad, but she wasn't completely defenseless. As

with most men, Pedro relied on his size to intimidate. However, her training with KM took that into account, and she didn't think herself too good to play dirty.

Pedro might smother her with his weight, but she was wiggly and tricky. She went for his eyes and ended up scratching his face. Her knee managed to wedge between them and press against his balls. But it was the headbutt into his nose that made him yelp and roll off her, cursing. "Fucking *puta*."

She didn't use the freedom to run. She reached for her gun and rose with it. "Yeah, I'm a bitch, asshole. You should have stayed away because now I'm gonna kill you, just like I killed your brother."

"Do it." Pedro held out his arms.

As if she would be that stupid. Killing Pedro in front of witnesses, especially since he made it look like he was giving up. Nope.

Instead, she moved away from him, passing by one of his thugs groaning on the field. The guy on the ground reached for her, so she kicked his hand and cast a smirk over her shoulder. "What's wrong? Ass too fat to catch a girl?"

"I am going to kill you with my bare hands," Pedro growled, lunging at her.

"I'd like to see you try." She darted away from him, then pretended to stumble. Then limp.

Let him think her weak and wounded. She pretended to limp away, moving for the dark recess across the street, past a few vehicles parked on the road.

In the distance, she could hear the wail of sirens. She didn't have much time. She slipped into the alley, hearing Pedro's heavy steps and labored breathing behind her.

Smoker lungs. It always gave them away.

She hid in the shadows, melded with them, and held her gun ready.

Pedro entered the alley, confident that he had her cornered. After all, it was a dead end. Only about eight feet across, not big enough for much but the dumpster at the very back, the rank smell enough to make Carla glad she hadn't eaten anything recently.

Pedro advanced on her, his gold tooth gleaming despite the sparse lighting. These warehouses had no windows facing the alley. No one to witness what she was about to do.

She held up the gun. "That's far enough. I'd rather not have your brains splatter my sweatshirt." It was a favorite.

"Your boyfriend's not here to save you, *puta*."

She snorted. "I don't need anyone to save me." She'd learned how to save herself a long time ago.

"You don't have the balls to fire."

"Don't need balls, just good aim." Carla's finger was on the trigger when she heard Philip say, "Put your hands on your head and get on your knees."

Seriously?

She barked, "I've got this, Moore. Just walk away."

"I can't let you kill him, Carla."

"He deserves it."

"I don't disagree, but you don't understand how killing a person can fuck you up. Trust me on this."

"You killed some people, *hombre?*" Pedro laughed as he turned. "A pussy gringo like you? Maybe I'll make you watch as I show your woman what a real man feels like—"

Bang.

Pedro didn't finish the sentence. Probably on account of the hole in his head. The man wavered on his feet for a moment and then toppled.

Her gun hadn't fired the killing shot.

She looked in disbelief at Philip. "I thought you didn't want me to kill him."

"I didn't. Which is why I handled it."

Sexy. So very sexy. "You're a killer."

He winced. "Yes, I guess you could say that but—"

"You don't have to explain or apologize." Carla stepped around the corpse and wrapped her arms around Philip. "I didn't mean that as a bad thing. I'm a killer, too."

"Carla—"

"No, really." She aimed her gun behind her and shot the corpse. "See. No problem at all."

His brow creased. "Wait a second, you mean all that joking around—"

"About being an assassin working on contract? Wasn't a joke." She grinned and shrugged. "Surprise."

A wry smile tugged his lips. "So, if I said I do vigilante jobs on the side, you wouldn't be offended?"

"More like turned on. Do you really kill bad dudes just for fun?"

His turn to look coy. "Just making the world a better place."

At the statement, she snorted. "Whatever turns your crank. I mostly do it for money. Or family. Or if they piss me off."

"So, in other words, stay on your good side."

"Smart soldier." She patted his cheek and yanked out her phone. She hit what at first appeared to be a game app—an alligator running around a sewer—but changed when she entered a numeric code.

"We should call for help," Philip stated.

"Help with what? He's dead. We need to get rid of the body before anyone sees it."

"We could always tell the cops it was self-defense."

She snorted. "And deal with the paperwork. Fuck that. I've got a better plan." Giving the phone one last look, she tucked it into a pocket. "Give me a hand. It's our lucky day." She moved to the dumpster at the far end of the dead-end alley. Philip didn't immediately follow, so she shoved at it alone. The damned trash container barely budged an inch.

"What are you doing?" Philip asked.

"Help me, and you'll see."

With the pair of them pushing and pulling, the dumpster moved, revealing a grate underneath. Carla knelt. "Help me pull it up."

"It will be bolted."

"What kind of Special Ops guy are you? Don't even have a multi-tool?"

"I'm a sniper. I shoot things."

"Then shoot."

"It will be loud."

"Which is why you'll wait for the whistle."

Before he could ask what whistle, the rumble of the approaching train filled the air and vibrated the alley. The wail of the whistle covered the blasts from his gun as Philip took out the bolts.

They had the grate moved, leaving an opening big enough to heave a body into, before the train finished passing. Philip insisted on dragging Pedro to the edge and shoving the body. It fell down the sewer hole and hit with a splash.

Philip looked at her, then the hole. "How did you know this was here?"

"I didn't. But I figured there was one nearby. City's got these storm sewers running all over, and I had them loaded into an app on my phone in case of emergency." Because an assassin never knew when she'd need a hole to bolt in or a good place to dump a body. "By the time Pedro is found, he'll be an unrecognizable mess."

"The blood in the alley..." He waved a hand at the spatter on the ground.

"Will be eliminated as soon as Meredith shows up with the bleach." She fired off a text as she spoke.

"You thought of everything. Will his death mean you and Nico are safe?"

She shrugged. "It was personal for Pedro. I doubt his friends will feel the same way." But just in case, she might have to move. Too many people knew about her house and identity.

Rather than saunter from the alley, she pulled a pin out of her key fob. She picked the lock of a door and led them into a storage room full of file folder boxes and office supplies.

"Where are we?"

"Mortgage broker office. Closed on Sundays. We can hang out for a bit while the heat dies down outside."

"Could take hours," he remarked.

"Only if Meredith or you killed any of them on the field."

"Nah, I made sure they were breathing, and they took off when they heard the cops."

"All of them?" she queried.

"As far as I know."

"Good, that means the cops will take some witness statements and then be on their way."

"They'll still want to talk to both of us."

"Probably." She shrugged. "They have to find us first. I plan to be long gone by tomorrow."

"You're leaving town? Going where?"

"Well that kind of depends on you," she boldly stated.

"Have you changed your mind about Pasadena?"

Her nose wrinkled. "No. But I might be persuaded to move nearby."

"What about Nico?"

"Nico will handle it. He won't have a choice. It's for his own safety." In the close confines of the storage closet, she tweaked his chin. "Play your cards right, soldier, and you'll get the same protection."

"I don't need you to protect me. I think you saw I am perfectly capable of taking care of myself."

"You are, which is nice. I'd hate to have to work, cook, clean, put out, and shoot the bad guys all on my own."

He snorted. "I must be dreaming. Because we are not having this conversation."

She grabbed him by the neck to haul him down for a kiss. A big kiss with tongue and heat. "Does that feel like a dream to you?" was her husky query.

Her phone buzzed.

"Must be Tanya. She was supposed to check in once she got Nico to safety."

"Hey, *chica*—" Carla felt the blood in her face drain as Tanya relayed in a gush of words what had happened. It was bad. "I'm coming right away. I'm in the money shark shop by the closed fish place." She hung up and moved from Philip back to the alley door. "We have to go.

"What happened?"

"It's Nico. He's missing."

"How is that possible? I saw him with Tanya before the fight started. She got him away from here."

But Carla wasn't listening. Couldn't with the panicked reminder of Tanya crying on the phone, "Someone took him, Carla. I'm so sorry."

Some asshole took her baby.

Uncaring if the cops were close by, Carla ran for the entrance of the alley and emerged in time to see the Mercedes screech to a halt.

"Get in," Meredith shouted through the window. Given Tanya was in the front, tissue held to her head—a fabric one because Merry was an old-fashioned kind of lady who had everything in her purse—Carla dove in the back, Philip beside her.

The car sped off. "What happened?" Philip asked while Carla took in details.

The blood and the blossoming bruise on Tanya's temple. The devastation on her face. The lack of Carla's son by her side.

"Where's Nico?"

Tanya's face crumpled. "I don't know. I was almost to the car with him when this guy came out of nowhere."

"Pedro's gang." Carla's lip curled.

Tanya shook her head and winced. "No. This guy was in a suit. Said he was under orders to take Nico to safety."

"Orders? Whose orders?"

"He didn't say. I told the jerk he couldn't have him."

"And he hit you?"

"Not exactly. I hit him first. I wasn't letting him touch Nico. So, I took him down and was about to slap the truth out of him when someone whacked me."

"He had an accomplice." Said grimly.

"I must have passed out. When I woke up, Nico was gone. I'm so sorry," Tanya sobbed.

Sorry? It wasn't Tanya's fault. Carla's blood ran cold, then hot.

Someone stole her son. *My precious. My baby.*

For that, they would die.

CHAPTER TWENTY-ONE

THE MOMENT PHILIP heard Tanya's story, a sinking sensation assailed him. He pulled his phone from his pocket and dialed.

No answer.

He dialed again.

It went to voicemail. He fired off a text.

Philip: *Where is the boy?*

Oliveira: *Safe.*

The confirmation from his boss both relieved and enraged Philip. He spat, "Nico's safe."

Carla whirled. "How do you know?"

Philip held up his phone, and she growled. Not the sexy growling sound she made in bed, but the rage of a mama bear unleashed.

"I will rip off his *cojones* with my bare hands and feed them to him. I will pull out his fingernails one by one, then stake him in a desert for the sun to bake him."

As Carla went on a litany of painful things, Philip texted his boss again.

Philip: *Bring him back.*

Oliveira: *Too late. He's on a plane to me. Bring his mother. I can explain.*

Leave it to Oliveira to have a private plane on standby.

Explain now, Philip texted.

No reply.

"I am going to kill that motherfucker," Carla yelled.

"Uh-oh," Meredith muttered.

"What is it?" Philip asked.

"Cops up ahead. They've got the road blocked."

"Shit." Philip grabbed the door handle.

"Where are you going?" asked Carla.

"I'll meet you at your house as soon as I can."

"Why leave? We can hide the guns." She popped hers into a compartment that blended seamlessly into the back of the driver side seat.

"No way am I getting through that roadblock," Philip said with a shake of his head. "They're gonna want me for questioning. I shot a guy."

"We got rid of Pedro's body."

"Not Pedro, the one before that. In the leg. In front of tons of witnesses.

"Oh, yeah. Think they know about it?"

"If they do, then they'll take all of us in for questioning. I doubt you want to wait that long. Wait for me at the house." He slipped out of the car. "I'll take a roundabout route back to you."

"I can't promise that."

"Carla." Philip added a warning tone to her spoken name. "Wait for me."

"I can't. I'm going."

He scrubbed a hand over his face. "Promise me one thing, don't kill him."

"I ain't making that promise. The man took my son. There have to be consequences."

Since he couldn't reason with Carla, Philip went after Meredith. "Don't let her go," he snapped. "Oliveira isn't a thug like Pedro. He's got guards. Well-trained ones. They're not going to let her waltz in and kill their boss."

"Don't worry about me, soldier. They'll never see me coming."

Before he could argue some more, Meredith hit the gas, and it was either try and run alongside or watch them leave.

They spent a few minutes at the roadblock. Then passed through. He, on the other hand, didn't.

"Hands on your head."

Lucky for him, the cops didn't shoot. But the questioning took hours.

By the time he made it back to Carla's house, she was long gone, and his boss still wasn't answering his phone.

CHAPTER TWENTY-TWO

IT TOOK hours of hard driving. Tanya switched in and out with Meredith so Carla could nap. Not that she managed much.

At least her friends understood her need for speed. A few days before, it had taken almost eight hours with Philip at the wheel. This time, just over six with speed and a lack of cops doing radar on their side.

Carla's anxiety was through the roof. She blamed herself.

Why didn't I protect Nico?

She'd let her desire to eliminate a threat leave her son vulnerable. She should have been by his side. How scared he must be. Was he hurt? Frightened?

As for Oliveira, what game did he play? Did he really think he could kidnap her son with impunity? Even he wasn't above the law.

If she chose to bring the law in to play.

She didn't. Oliveira had made this personal.

Arriving at the rich man's estate, Carla was tempted to march up to his gate and demand that he hand Nico over. However, KM hadn't trained an idiot.

Tanya was doing her thing and trying to get as much information about the layout and security as possible, while Meredith went for a late-evening jog, the rich bitch kind with designer clothes, perfect hair, and makeup that would withstand sweat. She would observe the gates into the place and then park her ass on the far side of the estate. Ready to infiltrate.

When Carla's phone rang—the tune Guns N' Roses', "Sweet Child o' Mine"—she knew she couldn't ignore it.

Carla answered the phone as she sat parked a street over from the estate. "Hello, Mother."

"Don't do it," said her handler, sounding frazzled.

"Do what? Kill the asshole who stole Nico?"

"That wasn't his fault. The men he sent to watch over you overstepped their bounds."

"He sent men to watch me?" The words were spoken flatly. "And you knew."

"Much has happened in the last twenty-four hours. There are things you don't know."

"Tell me."

"I can't. It's not my place. Go in and talk to Oliveira."

"Whose side are you on? Do you really expect me

to hand myself over, so Oliveira can make me disappear? He has my son."

"I know. But it's not what you think." Mother sighed. "Please, just trust me. Go and talk to him."

"Why should I listen to anything that man says?"

"Because I said so." An order from the boss, which only an idiot would ignore.

"I'm bringing my gun."

"Bring it. Just don't use it until he's said his piece."

"Maybe. I am making no promises." Carla hung up. "Did you find a weak spot in his security?" she asked Tanya.

"No. Why not go through the front door like Mother suggested."

Carla snorted. "As if. So? What's the verdict? Can I get in unseen?"

"Yeah. Here." Tanya pointed to a spot on a terrain map, the aerial view a sharp image of the property. "Scale the wall by this tree. Watch for the dude over here." She jabbed another section. "When he goes for his smoke, which happens every half hour, slip in."

"Seems too easy."

Tanya put her hand on Carla's arm. "Do you want me to come with you?"

"No." Left unsaid, "*This is my son. My duty.*"

"Then be careful."

Carla was super careful as she scaled the wall and sat on a tree branch. The irony of the camera sitting below her didn't escape her notice. She kept out of its line of sight and waited to spot the guard Tanya had told her about. Sure enough, he walked the perimeter of the wall, cigarette in hand. Sloppy. She smelled him before she even saw him, making him easy to avoid.

After he'd passed, she dropped from the tree and kept low to the ground. She used the bushes and shrubs in the garden to cover her approach. The open strip between the yard and the house gave her nowhere to hide, so she took a chance and sprinted across, plastering herself against the wall and inching along to the patio doors of the breakfast room. A quick peek inside showed it empty.

No Nico mowing down on waffles. Not even a platter of bacon. Shame. She could have used a slice right about now. Then again, it wasn't exactly breakfast time. Just before midnight, which meant most of the house would be asleep.

Even Nico.

Maybe after she'd rescued her son and sent Oliveira to meet his maker, they'd hit the nearest IHOP and fill up on pancakes smothered in syrup. Right after she hugged her boy hard enough to crack a few ribs.

Because she would find him. No way would Carla leave without Nico.

She inched in, holding her breath at the slight click when she shut the door. No sound of alarm. Weird. All that exterior protection and nothing on the doors.

She exited the breakfast room into an equally

empty hall, this time of the night not prone to much action. Given it was rather late, she assumed Oliveira was in bed. He'd get a rude awakening once she found him. The knife by her hip had a sharp edge.

As she went to ghost past the doors to his office, she noticed them open. Odd. When she'd stayed here before, they were always closed. To get to the stairs, she'd have to go past them.

A noise from the room let her know it was occupied.

She swung into the doorway, gun extended, not really caring who was in there. If staff, then they could take her to Oliveira. If it was the bossman himself, even better.

Oliveira sat in a chair in front of his desk, looking quite relaxed in a suit, no tie, top button of his shirt undone.

"Hello, Carla."

"Don't hello me, asshole. Where's Nico?"

"Upstairs. Sleeping."

She took a few steps forward, the barrel of her weapon aimed at his head. "You shouldn't have taken him."

"That was an accident. My men panicked when they saw the danger. I assure you, he's safe."

"I didn't ask how he was, I said give him back." Carla pressed the barrel against his forehead. "Now."

His expression remained placid. "So, the reports are true."

"What reports?"

"The ones I had compiled the first moment I saw you. Although, I didn't find out about your career until last night. An assassin for hire. That takes balls."

"It does. It also means I won't hesitate to pull the trigger."

"Did you know you're the spitting image of your mother?"

The subject change was abrupt, putting Carla off balance. "What the fuck? How would you know?" Even more disturbing, how had he gotten a picture of her mother?

"I knew her. Or should I say, my son did. Quite well, in fact. They were high school sweethearts until she moved away to America for a better life and married a man there."

"And? Do you really think I care if my mom dated your son? That doesn't give you the right to steal mine."

"I didn't mean to steal Nico, and you can leave with him at any time. I won't stop you."

He must lie. She meant to prove it and backed towards the door, waiting for him to make some kind of signal. Set off an alarm.

Instead, he said, "Did your mother ever tell you she returned for her sister's wedding? Arabella, I think was her name."

Carla shook her head. "I wasn't born yet when my aunt tied the knot."

"No, it happened about nine months before you

were born. Beautiful ceremony, I was told. My son Santos attended, as well."

At the words *nine months*, a roaring noise began to fill her head, making it hard to hear his next words.

"Santos and Juanita reconnected the week she visited. When the time came for her to leave, he begged her to stay. But she left. A week later, my son died in a car crash."

"The reports I read said he was drunk." Fast times led to an early demise.

"Drunk, yes, because he was grieving the loss of the woman he loved."

"Why should I care that your son and my mother had an affair?" She wanted him to say it. Say it aloud so she could deny it.

"Imagine my surprise when watching some videos, looking for potential academy recruits, I saw a boy who is the spitting image of my son. Further research showed that his mother looked just like the woman my Santos loved."

Carla shook her head. "I knew my father. He was a miserable, abusive drunk."

"No, he wasn't. Santos was a good man."

"You can't seriously think your son is my father."

"You left before the results came in." Oliveira pointed to an envelope on his desk. "I had a DNA test done. You are my granddaughter, and Nico, my great-grandson."

"No," Carla denied it. Couldn't listen to it.

Wouldn't believe it. Because if it were true...no, it changed nothing.

Oliveira was still a stranger who'd stolen her son.

Carla turned the barrel to point at Oliveira's head, just as Nico burst in yelling, "Mami, don't shoot."

CHAPTER TWENTY-THREE

PHILIP ARRIVED JUST BEFORE 10:00 a.m., the plane he'd chartered getting him there faster than by car, but the hours spent giving his statement to police meant that he was well behind Carla. A woman who wasn't answering his calls or texts.

Arriving at the mansion, Philip was somewhat relieved that he didn't see any flashing lights, not even those of an ambulance. The gate guards appeared relaxed and waved him through as if expecting him.

Still, when he pulled up to the front of the house, he imagined the worst. Either Carla had killed Oliveira, or his boss's guards had taken her out.

What he didn't expect was to see Nico in the far paddock, riding a pony with Oliveira and Carla standing side by side.

Something was wrong with this picture.

He exited the car and walked briskly in their direction. "Carla?"

"Hey, soldier. About time you got here. You missed all the excitement." Her bright smile took him aback.

"Is everything okay?" Philip asked, confused by the relaxed vibe. His hand dropped to his side and the piece he'd grabbed on his way over.

"I think so."

"More than okay." Oliveira beamed. "I'd like to formally introduce you to my granddaughter, Carlotta Oliveira."

"Granddaughter?"

"Long story."

"No shit. Are you sure?" Philip asked his boss.

"The blood doesn't lie."

"No, but you lied to me. Why not tell me?"

"Because I wanted to be sure." His boss shrugged. "This wouldn't be the first time I saw a boy who reminded me of Santos. I worried you'd think I was a crazy old man for even suspecting it was possible."

"Grandpa, look at me," Nico yelled as the pony went into a quicker trot.

"You are looking great, Nico." Oliveira moved away, and Philip sidled closer to Carla.

"So, it's true?"

"Apparently. My handler verified his claim."

"Doesn't make what he did right. Why not just fucking ask?"

"Because I would have run." Carla shrugged and

scuffed the ground with her shoe. "My past is something I buried a long time ago. Any mention of it would have sent me into hiding with Nico."

"Still..." Philip frowned at Oliveira, who chatted with Nico, looking happier than Philip had ever seen.

"I know. I'm still weirded out, as well." She leaned against the fence and stared at him. "Did you know he's been watching me for weeks?"

He frowned. "No. I guess he hid that from me, too. Why did it take him so long to figure it out?"

"For one thing, Carla Baker wasn't the name I was born with. I left that name when I escaped Matias and my old life. So, Luiz's initial research hit a dead end because he couldn't figure out who Carla Baker was."

"You assumed a new identity."

"My agency set it up. Just like my agency muddled all trails leading to me. When Luiz began poking around, Mother sent a subtle warning to stop."

"Hold on, I thought your mother was dead."

"She is. The *Mother* I'm talking about is my handler."

He scrubbed his face. "This is complicated."

"I'm almost done. So, anyhow, given the threat, he thought it was a good idea to send you out to see if you could convince me to show up."

"Why not just contact you himself?"

"Because he still wasn't sure. He was having a hard time getting DNA samples. I'm a bit of a freak when it comes to wiping my traces. I don't even put garbage on the curb. I wasn't as careful when we were staying here, and Luiz got what he needed to run the tests."

"I still don't understand why he didn't say anything to me," Philip grumbled. "I've been working for him for years."

"As his right-hand man and killer. You were his backup plan."

He gave her a sharp look. "Hold on, he sent me out there to kill you?" Because Oliveira never mentioned the possibility to him.

"Not me. After Mother threatened Luiz, he thought I might be involved in something bad. Mob. Drugs. Bad shit that might require me to assume another identity. He sent you to extricate me from a sticky situation if needed."

"Fine, let's say I'm following this convoluted soap opera. Why kidnap Nico?"

"Total accident. He was having some private investigators watch me. They saw the brawl happening and thought they'd earn brownie points by spiriting Nico to safety."

"You didn't wait for me," was Philip's reply to that.

"Nico needed me."

"Do you have any idea how worried I was?"

"I didn't kill anyone," Carla said with a smirk.

"I was worried about you, nitwit. You should have waited for me so we could do this as a team."

She laced her arms around his neck. "Speaking of team, remember how I said I was relocating? I found a spot. Although, it might be temporary. I told Luiz I'd stick around so we could see if we can tolerate each other."

"He's your family."

"We'll see about that."

"What about your job?"

"My insurance company will transfer me if I ask."

"I meant your other job."

She smiled. "Way I hear it, you could use a partner."

"Not just for work," he noted, lacing his arms around her. "I like you Carla, Carlotta, or whatever name you want to use."

"I like you, too, Philip." One of the rare times she addressed him by his name, but it was the kiss she placed on his lips that meant the most.

Because it was in front of her son who yelled, "Eww. Gross. They're kissing."

They did more than kiss when Philip snuck into her room that night.

The moment he entered, Carla spun him into the wall, and her body crowded his.

"Took you long enough," she grumbled.

"Oliveira kept me talking in his office. I think he was hoping I'd forget about visiting you." As if he could stay away. The hard length of his cock pressed against her lower belly.

"Think he'll rush in with a shotgun and order you out?"

"I'll shoot him if he does," Philip murmured as he laced his fingers through hers and kept her close enough to kiss.

"I'll find a shovel if it's necessary."

"You are so fucking crazy perfect," he murmured against her mouth.

"So crazy I'll kill you if you ever screw me over."

"Then I'd better do my best to make you happy." He flipped their positions so that her cheek was against the wall and her ass facing him. The minx squirmed, rubbing herself against his erection.

He curved a hand around her waist and encouraged her butt to arch in invitation.

He shoved her pants down. Panties, too, baring her to his view. His touch.

He ran a hand down her hip, and she wiggled.

"What are you waiting for?"

"Say you're my girlfriend."

"Why the fuck would I do that?" She cast him a coy look over her shoulder.

He slid a hand between her legs, stroked her, watched her eyes dilate and heard her breathing hitch. "Because I don't want to be a dirty secret."

"I kissed you in front of Nico."

"You did," he acknowledged, "and now you're going to say it. You're my girlfriend."

"You're my girlfriend," she parroted, then laughed on a gasp as he slapped her ass.

"Try again," he said, grinding himself against her, his lips against the shell of her ear.

"I'm your girlfriend." The words spoken breathlessly.

"Was that so hard?"

Her ass rubbed against him as she replied, "It is very hard."

Hard and ready. Philip nudged her legs apart, spreading them for his touch. He fingered her as his free hand unzipped his pants.

He traced her damp slit, parting her nether lips, dipping into the honeyed heat. He slid the finger deep, then added a second, penetrating her. Feeling her tightness, the wetness. The desire...

She responded to his touch, moaning, trembling. Her breathing grew shallow as he pumped her with his fingers and, in reply, she rocked back against him. He stroked her over and over, building her pleasure, feeling her tighten with each deep thrust.

When he couldn't stand it anymore, he dropped to his knees, and she let out a cry of loss as his fingers slipped away only to be replaced by his tongue.

With sinuous pleasure, he traced her sex, slipping his tongue between her nether lips, probing her before flicking the tip against her clit. She cried out and bucked as he sucked at her, teased her. He worked her sensitive button until she quivered and panted, "Fuck me. Philip. Please."

His sweet killer, begging?

Rather than stop, he kept tonguing her, increasing her pleasure until she came, a low moan rolling out of her as her body clenched and shook.

And still, he kept licking. Stroking. Working her until she began to moan and rock again. Only then did he stand and thrust into her, his cock more than ready to fill her sex. It was decadently blissful, her channel still vibrating with the aftershocks of her orgasm. Fisting him tightly. He dug his fingers into her flesh as he began to move inside that tight sheath. Pushing and pulling against the suction. His thick shaft stretched her. Pummeled her g-spot until she was gasping and holding on to the wall for dear life.

There was no breath for words. Nothing but the decadent sensation of his prick sliding in and out, her pussy gripping him tightly, increasing the pleasure. As his pace quickened, he was soon slapping in and out of her, the rigid length of his cock filling her. She was on the edge of coming again, he could feel it. She just needed a little push.

He reached around and fondled her clit, pinching it. She bucked. Her sex clamped down, and she cried out, "Fuck me, yes!" as her second orgasm hit hard.

"Yes, yes," he hissed along with her as he kept thrusting until his own orgasm hit, a hot blast that left him limp, shuddering, and wrapped around her, whispering, "I think I fucking love you."

For a second, she stiffened. Softened. Then she was Carla. "Why did you have to go and say that?"

"Because you're wicked and amazing."

"I'm a killer mom who drives a minivan."

"Like I said, amazing." He flipped her around so she faced him. "I don't expect you to say it back. Just expressing what I feel."

"Love is weak?" she said, the words sounding more question than statement.

"Then it's a good thing you're around to protect me."

"Idiot. Kiss me again." He kissed her and made love to her, and while she might not be able to spit out the words, she showed her affection in the way she kept him in her bed that night and only kicked him out at dawn.

Whispering, "See you later, boyfriend."

EPILOGUE

A FEW WEEKS LATER...

The move from her townhouse to Pasadena passed without a hitch. Mother made most of the arrangements. The Carla Baker that used to work at an insurance agency disappeared. Nico's records were erased. While Pedro might be dead—and his body still yet to be found—there was no point taking any chances.

Carlotta started over, and while she didn't take Luiz's last name, she compromised and went back to her mother's maiden one.

Nico made the move without protest. He was already enrolled in the academy and loving his new life. Not only had he made some friends, he also thrived under the bond forming between him and Luiz.

The relationship between Carla and Luiz was a bit

more cautious and strained. He kept wanting to spoil her. She didn't trust it and kept refusing gifts. Except for one.

The coach house on her grandfather's estate was a compromise. It gave her the space she needed, while at the same time, making him feel better about having his only family nearby.

It still amused her to no end that he took issue with the fact that Philip spent many nights with her. When Oliveira threatened to fire him for messing with his granddaughter, Philip resigned.

Oliveira rehired him for more money rather than see him headhunted by a rival. And Philip continued his quest to rid the world of bad shits. Although, he took offense at her calling him Dexter.

As to her side job with KM? While Carla still kept in touch with Mother and her sisters, she'd retired.

More or less.

Philip's hobby inspired her. Given her past, she developed a new calling, helping battered women get away from their abusers. And if those abusers wouldn't let go...their accidental deaths appeared as fortuitous coincidence.

All in all, life was good. She still drove a minivan, the must-have for any soccer mom. Her son was safe and, best of all, he'd given Carla permission, whispering to her as he saw Philip's car pull in for the sixth time that week, "I like him. He'd make a good Papi." Nico shoved something into her hand.

She looked at the object in consternation: a plastic ring, still sticky from the caramel popcorn box he'd likely pulled it from.

When Philip walked in with his sexy, "Hey, hot stuff. How was your day?"

She blurted, "Will you marry me?" Then groaned. "Shoot me."

"I'd rather marry you." Said a moment before he sealed the promise with a kiss.

Later that night, when he held her in his arms, and she thought he was asleep, she finally said it.

"I love you."

Then punched him as he channeled Han Solo and said, "I know."

Tanya read the online invitation and snorted.

Her son caught the sound and said, "What's up, Mom?"

"Aunt Carla is getting hitched."

"To a wagon?" her son the smarty-pants asked.

"No, silly, to a man."

"Are we gonna go? I wanna see Nico."

"I don't see why not. It's after your tournament in Quebec." That happened to coincide with an easy spying gig that Mother had landed Tanya.

What she didn't expect was to run into Cory's

daddy while she was there...

Looking for more Eve Langlais romantic suspense?

Check out Bad Boy Inc.

CPSIA information can be obtained
at www.ICGtesting.com
Printed in the USA
BVHW030851060519
547451BV00001B/54/P

9 781773 840642